SHINE ON, LUZ VÉLIZ!

Shine On, Luz Véliz!

Rebecca Balcárcel

chronicle books
san francisco

Library of Congress Cataloging-in-Publication
Data available.

ISBN 978-1-7972-0967-8

Manufactured in China.

Design by Jay Marvel.
Typeset in Fazeta and Mabry Mono Pro.

10 9 8 7 6 5 4 3 2 1

Chronicle Books LLC
680 Second Street
San Francisco, California 94107

Chronicle Books—we see things differently.
Become part of our community at www.chroniclekids.com.

To Azucena, my Guatemalan sister,
a luz and a sol for me and this world

"We are very, very small, but we are
profoundly capable of very, very big things."

—Stephen Hawking

So there's before it happened. Before I learned to use crutches. Before I needed physical therapy. Before, before, before.

Welcome to After.

I grab a trash bag that's almost as tall as I am. LAWN AND LEAF, the box says. Perfect for raking out the whole soccer section of my closet. Perfect for clearing out Before.

Soccer shoes? Into the bag. Shin guards? Into the bag. White-and-blue uniforms? The bag. Three trophies, one for being the top scorer in the whole Tri-Cities Junior League? Bag. I can't look at this stuff anymore.

Then there's the ball. Am I keeping it? No way.

Well?

No.

Okay, fine. I can't let go of my soccer ball yet.

I'm not supposed to dribble it in the house, but I pop it into the air with the toe of my shoe and bounce it on my good knee. The knee that bends easy as a Slinky. Clean joint, perfect tendons. I'm thankful for one healthy knee. Really, I am. But I'm sad, too. I used to have two of them.

I shove the ball to the very back of my closet, behind a wall of cardboard bricks I used to make forts with.

Now for the posters of my soccer heroes.

I yank out each pushpin. Down falls Abby Wambach, top scorer of the US Women's Team. Down goes the World Cup team photo, every neck with a gold medal, and captain Megan Rapinoe raising the trophy high. I crumple the posters into big wads and stuff them into the trash bag.

Mom says to stop looking back, so here I am trying, but it's hard to forget. Sometimes I flash into the past. A memory will photobomb my brain. Like that run. That last-day-on-the-soccer-field run.

It plays over and over in my head, a YouTube video on continuous autoplay. Legs pumping, feet churning up the grass, my body a missile speeding toward the goal . . .

I know the accident happened. Obviously. But at the same time, it's like I'm still running. The goal getting closer, and Mom cheering in the stands. Dad shouting, "Pour it on!" which makes me run even faster.

Some "me" kept on running, but I couldn't go with her. It's like she went on without me, to where I was supposed to go. Now we'll never find each other.

Instead of scoring, I felt a leg sweep under me, my body spinning backward, the blur of another jersey, and pain spiraling out from my knee and ankle. Doctors would later tell me my anterior cruciate ligament tore, my shin broke, and my patella fractured. All I knew then was a dark tunnel, my vision gone, and the screaming pain growing louder.

So maybe I am almost used to it now. The leg, I mean. The pain meds and the therapy and the discussions about whether to do surgery. At least I can walk. No more crutches or canes. I'm left with a "wobbly" knee, they say.

Which means I can't play soccer this spring—or maybe ever. I lost the thing I was best at. The thing that filled three evenings a week and Saturday mornings; gave me automatic friends, at the local league and at school. The thing that made me special.

Now I'm plain Luz. Bran muffin girl instead of blueberry cinnamon.

And now Mom and Dad freak out if I race someone to the bus or charge up stairs two at a time or even walk fast, if you can believe it. They say my knee could "give."

So yeah, I'm getting used to the knee. The thing that bothers me is Dad. He hardly talks to me anymore. It's like he can't get over it. I guess I'm not surprised. He coached me my whole life. I held a soccer ball before I held a spoon, they tell me. Eleven years is a long time, even to a grown-up.

I haul my trash bag of soccer stuff to the living room, where Dad's up a ladder, putting a new light fixture on the ceiling fan. Does he see me at all?

"Can I help?" I ask. "Maybe hand you some tools?" I'm kind of good at mechanical things. I installed my own kitty-cat light-switch plate, and I can build anything from LEGO bricks, with or without the directions.

"All I need is this screwdriver," he says.

"Can I just watch?" I say, remembering how he used to let me help replace a door handle or change a light bulb.

"If you really want to, Lucita."

Which is my nickname. He doesn't say it with a smile, though, and my heart wilts a little. He doesn't notice the trash bag in my hands, though it's right in front of me and big as a Texas sage bush.

Before, before, before, he was the head coach of Tri-Cities Youth Soccer. After, after, after, he's just Dad the landscaper. He quit coaching the day I got hurt; another parent took over. He works his landscaping design business, Véliz Verde, even on Saturdays now.

So fine. I didn't want to help with some old ceiling fan anyway.

I pull on my red jacket and head outside with the trash bag. My plan? Put my soccer life on the curb, let the garbage truck haul it away, and dump the past into the past.

"Luz!" Mom shouts. "Be careful on the driveway."

Be careful, be careful, be careful. *I know.*

I face sideways and take our super-steep drive-way slowly, good leg first. I hoist the trash bag with both hands. It lands with a satisfying thump.

A voice carries from across the street. "A little early for trash day." It's Mr. Mac, pulling winter covers off his bushes. He points to his wristwatch as he says "a little early," but his eyes smile.

"Yup," I say.

"Never known you to be early. Must be important. Or smelly!"

That's what I like about Mr. Mac. He figures you know what you're doing. He figures you've got your reasons.

Mr. Mac isn't his full name. It's Mr. MacLellan, but we're buddies, so I get to say Mr. Mac. He was the first neighbor we met when we moved in, and guess what he brought as a welcome gift? Not cookies, not tuna casse-role, not some boring welcome card. He brought a lamp that turns on when you clap. It also works when I snap. Practically magic!

Mom calls him Gadget Santa because he's always giving us gadgets, like a motion detector that chimes when Zigzag goes out her cat door. Plus Mr. Mac knows stuff. When I graduated from crutches, he showed me *his* banged-up knee and how to use a cane.

Turning my back on the trash bag, I call over, "It *is* important. It's my old soccer stuff."

He nods his hatted head, and the sun glints off his round glasses. He's quiet for a second. "That's a prickly one to swallow, all right."

It sure is. It won't be easy looking at my bare bedroom, but it's better than looking at a room that makes me sad. "That's a fact," I say.

"Do you remember Stephen Hawking, Luz?"

"The physics guy who talked through a computer?"

"That's him. He said something about intelligence. And he was a smart guy. Test scores, or even high grades— that's not what intelligence is. Hawking says, it's being able to adapt to change."

I let that sink in. "You mean my leg?" I glance at my trash bag. "So is this me, um, 'adapting to change'?"

"As best you can, right? And life *is* change, I've found." He resets his hat, which has a solar-powered fan built into the top. "Not that it's easy, of course."

I think about the soccer ball still in my closet, and I know that I'm not all the way adapted. Of course, I might play around with the ball again, just for fun. But what if being a star was what made it fun? And Before Dad showing me his soccer secrets, which After Dad doesn't do. I'm not sure soccer can ever be fun now.

Mr. Mac points to his open garage. "Look what I found," he calls.

He picks up a large remote, extends the antenna, and a red toy car zips out. I love that little thing. Little Red, we call it. He lets me drive it sometimes. Now it crosses the street, zooms right to my feet. Welded to the roof is a shallow box, kind of a tray. Mr. Mac made that part himself. Inside the box tray sits a black electronic device—maybe an old, old phone?

I turn it over in my hands. Rectangular buttons line one edge, four black and one red.

"Explore it. See what you can make of it," Mr. Mac says, zooming Little Red and its empty tray back across the street.

"Will do!" I give him a wave and climb back up the driveway, turning the mystery object over in my hand.

Mom meets me at the door. "What do you have there?"

"I don't know." I push one of the buttons and a whole side of the device springs open.

"I haven't seen one of those in a long time," she says.

"Mr. Mac said to explore it."

"Mr. MacLellan's always got something interesting for you, doesn't he?" Mom says, pointing at my bare head. She always wants me to wear a hat if it's the least bit sunny.

I ignore her gesture and hang my jacket on its hook.

"So, come here a minute. We need to talk."

"What about?" I say, pressing another button on the black thingamajig.

She disappears into the house, her words fading as she goes. "We'll talk about it as a family."

As a family? There's only three of us. Mom, Dad, and me. What's the big deal? This is not what I want to do with my Sunday afternoon.

From the black gadget, I pull out a plastic rectangle—sort of a cartridge. It has two holes in it, with tiny teeth, like gears. "Can this talk-meeting-thing wait?" I call as I head toward my bedroom.

"No, Luz," Mom says from the kitchen. "Dad's already in the dining room."

I set the black device on my bedside table and turn back. Then I stop. I stand at my bedroom doorway. I let a second go by. Then two.

Dad's been so quiet lately. So gone all the time. So busy, busy, busy. Part of me wants to stand here and make him wait. Make him think about me. Make him wonder where I am and if I'm okay. But of course he knows I'm in my room. He knows I'm basically okay.

Except I'm not.

I plop myself down in a wooden chair at the dining table. I'm guessing Mom set up this meeting, because Dad's clearly not into it. He's fidgeting, reaching for his phone, then pulling his hand back. Somehow the air feels crackly. Zigzag is nowhere nearby; she's probably lazing on a pile of warm laundry.

Mom leans toward me. "I had a call from the school counselor."

My whole body tenses. Ms. Martin? *Am I in trouble?*

"She just needs to know whether to keep soccer on your schedule for the last nine weeks of school."

Whoa, whoa, whoa. I lean back. If I know one thing, it's that I'm staying in Athletic Hour even if I'm not playing. I like getting outside, smelling the grass. Watching how the ball rolls and rolls and never gets tired.

Dad blows air with puffed cheeks. His eyes look red around the rims. Does it make him *that* sad that I'm not playing soccer right now? Or fútbol, as he calls it when we're watching a match on the Spanish-language station. He used to whistle as he kneed the soccer ball up and bounced it off his chest, keeping it in the air for minutes. He'd grin when I outran a defender on the field or when I cheered our favorite players on TV. These days, he seems to have two settings: quiet and sad.

Mom goes on. "She said you can stay in soccer if you want. It's not a problem with your grade or anything. Now that you're off the cane, Coach will give you things to do."

Wait a second. Things? "Like pass out water bottles?" I ask. Suddenly I remember the girl who used to do that. I don't think I talked to her before she switched to a different class. Maybe she felt left out? I'm not sure why she was there, actually.

"Or maybe something more interesting?" Mom's face looks hopeful. She's got her look-on-the-bright-side eyebrows going on.

"Everyone I know is in soccer," I say. That's the main thing, right? Although I wouldn't call them friends. I mean, we're sort of *all* friends, but I don't go over to their houses or anything. And in Athletic Hour they're on the field the whole time, and I'm—well, *not*. Not anymore.

"It doesn't matter to us," Mom says, looking at Dad for confirmation, who doesn't respond. Doesn't he care what happens?

Anyway, I don't believe her. I *know* it matters to them. I'll never forget the first time I scored a winning goal. I was only five, but I knew I'd done something special. They were on their feet, shouting, "That's our girl!" I haven't felt that glow since I left the field.

"You *could* take another class." Mom searches my face for the answer, but I don't have one yet.

"Like what?" I've never thought about any electives but soccer.

"Ms. Martin has some ideas. Photography, art. Or what about band? You could dust off your trumpet."

I try not to roll my eyes, but I can't help it. Mom's a band director, so she thinks everyone loves music. I like hearing it, but playing it? Not so much. I quit trumpet two years ago.

"Let Luz do what she wants," Dad breaks in.

"Of course," says Mom, glaring at him. "That's why we're sitting here."

Dad sighs and runs his hand through his hair. I wonder what he's thinking. Is he annoyed this might break my last link to soccer? Or does he want to jump in and say something but can't? Why is he making Mom handle it all?

This isn't the first time they've growled at each other. Something's off between them recently. They think I don't notice, but they misunderstand each other more, like they're on the same team but executing two different plays. They talk in sharp voices behind their bedroom door, and when they come out, Dad's too quiet. Some kind of softness between them has stiffened, like when taffy gets cold in the refrigerator. Instead of stretching, it can snap.

Now it seems like it doesn't matter if I stay in soccer class or not. Somehow, Dad not fighting for it makes me want to give up, too. Everyone knows I'll just be putting in the time. Getting an A for showing up. I can't picture Dad high-fiving me for *that* kind of A.

Mom leans in farther, pulling my gaze to her. "For tomorrow, go to soccer. Ms. Martin says you can change your schedule all the way up until Friday if you want to."

Mom's trying, I'll give her that. I can tell she wants me to be happy. But she also wants life to flow like one of her symphonies. Everything timed right, everything harmonizing. My accident threw in a bunch of wrong notes. She keeps trying to fix it, but let's face it: We haven't found the new song yet. Nothing's like it was.

I slouch to my room and look at the empty walls. The truth is, I thought I'd play soccer forever. At least make the high school team someday. Earn one of those letter jackets maybe? I know now that can't happen. Yet I always planned to stay in the class. . . .

Maybe that was dumb.

Or maybe it's dumb to think I'd fit in anywhere else.

If my brain were a dump truck, I'd raise the dump bed high and let a bunch of stuff slide out: soccer, the school counselor, the family meeting, and Dad acting half bored, half angry. I'd leave it all in a big pile and drive away.

Instead I perch on the edge of my bed and pick up the black thing Mr. Mac sent over by remote-controlled car. Maybe this will clear my head.

A lump moves under my covers. It's Zigzag. As usual, she's burrowed to the middle of the mattress, taking up all the room. "Can I borrow your bed?" I say, teasing her. She meows before settling back into her nap.

I turn over the device in my hands. It's about as heavy as a phone, but bulkier. The buttons look like a row of Starburst candies standing on edge, except their color. The writing has almost worn off, but I make out PLAY, FF, REW, STOP, and next to the red one, REC.

REC has got to mean record. I press it and say, "Testing. Testing. This is Luz Véliz, formerly of Tri-City Soccer League." But when I press PLAY, no sound plays back. The little wheels spin silently inside the cartridge. I check the volume, turning the dial all the way up. Still nothing.

What are the other buttons? I open my laptop and Google REW. It stands for "Roblox Extreme Wrestling." I press REW anyway. Now the wheels spin backward until I press STOP.

This time, PLAY sends my voice into the room. Yes! I rush down the hall and out the door, one arm in my jacket. "Be right back!" I call.

"Okay, but we're about to eat supper," Mom says. "Your dad's got veggie patties on the grill."

Mmm, that actually sounds good. Maybe he's trying to improve the afternoon. "I'll be quick!" I sidestep down the steep driveway, happy to see that Mr. Mac's still out, his garage door open.

"It's a tape recorder!" I shout, holding it high.

Mr. Mac claps. "You figured it out!"

A warmth builds behind my ears and spreads to the top of my head. I can't suppress my smile.

"Soccer's not your only skill, you see."

"I hope you're right." I really mean it.

"Of course! You'll be good at many things. Many things. And . . ."—he taps his cane on the ground for emphasis—"being good at things isn't what really matters anyway."

"But it is." Isn't that the only way to feel good? To get noticed?

He shakes his head.

"Okay, Mr. Mac, you got me." I'm pretty sure he's wrong, but I know what he wants me to ask. "What *does* matter?"

"Just being Luz in the world."

He says it like it's the key to everything, but I gotta say, I always thought being Luz meant kicking a ball. *Luz in the world.* I'm not sure how I can— "Hey, are you making a joke? Loose in the world?"

"Haha! Not on purpose, but I like it. You're loose in the world. Maybe you can 'let loose'?"

"Loosen up?" I add.

"Good one!" Mr. Mac's chuckle builds to laugh. I've heard these before, but making him laugh makes them funny.

I take a seat on a stool at Mr. Mac's long wooden worktable. The whole place looks like an electronics store, with computers along one wall. A lot of them are old, like museum-old. Screens as boxy as dog crates.

I hand over the tape recorder, and Mr. Mac pops out the cartridge. He points to one edge. "See this black strip?" he says. "It's magnetic tape. A plastic strip covered in magnetic particles."

I look at the cartridge with more respect.

"When you press record, the machine converts audio signals into magnetic energy. When you play it back, the imprinted signal is changed into electrical energy and amplified."

"Wow." I'm not sure what all of that means, but it sounds cool. "They knew a lot back in your day." I feel my eyes go wide as it dawns on me that I probably just insulted him.

Mr. Mac laughs. "We knew a thing or two, all right. I was about your age when this cassette recorder came along. I recorded myself playing the banjo."

It's my turn to laugh. I can't picture Mr. Mac playing an instrument. "Did you really play the banjo?" I ask.

"*Did* I? Still do, now and again. You could say I know my way around that truck stop." Mr. Mac walks deeper into the garage. "Come on back," he says, and I follow. The place looks like what I imagine the basement of Google would, or a storage room at NASA. I always love the smell, a mix of rubber and WD-40, maybe from the bicycle hanging from hooks in the ceiling.

We walk down the row of old computers. A poster hangs over each one. Scientists. I recognize Stephen Hawking in his wheelchair. He was into physics. The three women are Katherine Johnson, Rosalind Franklin, and Marie Curie. I've looked them up before. NASA math, DNA, and radioactivity.

Farther back, green boards with silvery circuits lean against one another on a shelf. Cables hang in neat loops from nails. Cabinets line the back wall, with labels like SOLDERING IRON and FLOPPY DISKS.

Mr. Mac pulls out a drawer, revealing a whole collection of tape recorders. One is the size of a hardcover book, while another is as small as a flip phone. Mr. Mac picks up the small one. "Uses a microcassette, this one does." He presses a button, and a one-inch cassette pops out. "You know, early home computers stored programs on tape recorders."

He's like my own personal History Channel. "They did?"

"You'd have your screen, your keyboard, and one of these." He taps the largest tape recorder. "Without that, your data erased every time you turned off the computer."

Whoa, that would be a pain.

"Luz!" Mom's voice carries into the garage, faint but definite.

"I gotta go," I say. "Thanks for showing me . . . well, everything."

"Anytime, Luz."

On my way up the driveway, I see Mom waving at Mr. Mac. "Don't let her bother you too much, Mr. MacLellan," she says.

"No bother, Ms. Véliz. Smart cookie you have there!"

"We'll bring over some lentil soup soon."

"That's my favorite," Mr. Mac says.

Mom worries about Mr. Mac eating right. He always talks about his microwave popcorn, but that's not healthy enough in Mom World. It's easy to make, though, and he looks okay to me. I think he's just efficient.

"How's your mail-alert system working?" he asks.

"Like a charm!" Mom says. "The light bulb burned out the other day, but we replaced it. What are you going to invent next?"

"Oh, I have a project on hand. A little something for my grandson."

I wonder what it is. Maybe a doorbell that roars like a dinosaur? Or a device that measures how far you've ridden your bike. "Will you show me, Mr. Mac?"

"Happy to, Luz. Next time."

I hope next time is soon.

From the driveway, I can smell the veggie patties grilling. I hope this means a nice night with no talk of soccer or the counselor or whatever Mom and Dad have been annoyed about recently. Tomorrow is Monday, and I have soccer first thing. That's drama enough.

The next morning, soccer basically stinks. No one in the class looks at me like I'm important. In fact, they mostly ignore me. Even Skyler, who was my closest thing to a friend in here, is too busy to talk. We used to size up the opposing team over warm-ups and race each other down the sidelines. Now she waves to me as she runs onto the field.

On Tuesday, it's the same.

On Wednesday? I'm not expecting much. When I had my cast and crutches, sure, I was a celebrity. The whole team buzzed around me. What's the inside of an ambulance look like? Did it hurt to get a cast put on? Can I try your crutches? Fangirl, fangirl, fangirl.

Now I *look* recovered, which is to say, Not Interesting Anymore. But my knee and ankle aren't strong. I'm not supposed to risk running, stopping fast, turning, or twisting yet. "One good twist and you'll be back in a brace, young lady," the doctor said. So now I don't carry around the prop of an Injured Person, but the damage is still there.

Everyone starts suiting up in the locker room. On my way to change clothes, Coach Schubert stops me. "You can dress out if you want, but you don't have to."

"Aren't I supposed to?" I've been dressing out ever since the cast came off.

She shrugs. "I wouldn't. I should have mentioned it before. Sorry about that." She rushes off with her clipboard, already needed outside.

I sit down on the cold metal bench, my eyes drawn to the drain in the middle of the concrete floor.

"Hey, I'll come check on you out there," Skyler says, jogging past.

It's nice, but she said the same thing yesterday and forgot. I don't blame her. She has drills to do, after all, and scrimmages to play. I think of how she asked me to a movie once, and I didn't go. I watched a big game with Dad instead. Maybe she gave up on me after that.

My stomach knots up as the locker room empties. This whole sidelines gig didn't bother me as much before, but now I see that it might never get better.

I look over at the crate of water bottles. I *could* roll it out to the field. Maybe I could bring out some towels, too, for wiping off sweat?

Being the water girl is nothing like being the high-scorer. I can't imagine my parents saying, "That's our girl!" for handing out Ozarka.

"Hey, what are you waiting for?" The assistant coach passes me and grabs the handle of the water crate. Suddenly, getting out there and smelling the grass doesn't sound so good. Grass is the smell of everything I can't do anymore.

"Can I go to the nurse?" I squeak.

She steps toward me and squints at my face. "You do look a little pale. What's bothering you?"

I mumble something about my stomach, and she writes me a pass.

Stepping into the hall is a relief. I can breathe better. Out here, I'm not the only screw in a box of nails. *Just think,* I tell myself, *every one of these classrooms is filled with kids who are not playing soccer right now either.* I try to forget the coaches and the team. Forget the grass, the ball, the beauty of a completed pass.

I miss it. And I really miss hearing Dad tell his friends, "My girl, what speed she has!"

My tennis shoes squeak on the shiny floors. The hall feels wider than usual, the ceiling higher, I guess because it's empty. I walk in the direction of the nurse, but I take the long way.

The hallway dead-ends in a T intersection. I'm about to turn left, but a thumping noise makes me look right.

The last room's door is propped open, and not with a wooden wedge or a brick. A replica of R2-D2 stands against the door, its red light glowing. Okay, I'll bite.

The thumping noise continues, and I step toward the room. At the doorway, I poke my head in, hoping to get a peek without being noticed.

The kids aren't sitting at desks. They're walking around. They seem tall—probably seventh or even eighth graders. Some carry LEGO bricks and gears in their hands. Some lean over a couple of computers along the back wall. A blue mat stretches across the floor, and on it, two robots roll toward a line of Ping-Pong balls.

I forget to hide and step into the room, my eyes fixed on the rolling robots. The thumping I heard was their metal arms hitting the mat, trying to trap a Ping-Pong ball.

One boxy robot has rubber bands wrapped around plastic circles to serve as tires. The other has a caterpillar design that reminds me of an army tank. Both try to catch the balls in nets.

"Why won't it turn?" says a ponytailed girl as the tank bot gets stuck in a corner.

"We need a bigger net," says a red-shirted boy gripping a control box attached by a long cord to the wheeled bot. "What if we had a scoop instead?"

Right then, he looks up and meets my eyes. His bot runs into a wall, and he shouts, "Ms. Freeman!"

A woman with close-cropped hair and a multicolored dress sweeps toward me. "Well, hello!" She looks over my head and down the hall, maybe expecting to see the rest of my class or an adult. "Can I help you?"

I don't want to say that I'm lost. I don't want to say that I'm running away from what used to be my favorite class. I start talking, even though my mind is a blank screen. "I was just, uh . . ." *Think think think!* "What is this class?"

Ms. Freeman takes note of my hall pass before answering. "Robotics. Robotics Two, actually."

"It looks seriously cool."

"What you're seeing took a lot of work. It starts at the computer." She gestures toward the students along the back wall. "There's design, programming, and finally testing. We discover first, then create."

I nod, still watching the two bots. One has managed to capture a ball, but it can't catch a second one without the first one escaping. I think of Little Red, Mr. Mac's remote-controlled car. I wonder if Mr. Mac has ever designed a robot.

"How do you get in this class?" I hear myself say. "Hypothetically."

"Hypothetically?" She smiles. "Are you a sixth grader?" Seeing my nod, she shakes her head. "These students took a semester of Intro to Robotics and a semester of Robotics One. To take this class next year, you should be in Robotics One now."

"Soccer is my elective this year." I say this quietly.

"You can start the sequence next year."

"Go through another whole school year first?" That sounds long. Way too long.

Ms. Freeman's eyes almost smile. "Listen, I have to get back to my students, but I have an idea. If you need an elective, the fifth graders have a first-period Intro to Robotics over at the elementary school. You could probably jump into that now and get started, at least."

"Fifth graders?" My voice comes out louder than I meant it to. This is a definite drawback to having the elementary school across the street. I don't want to go backward.

Ms. Freeman doesn't respond to my shock. "Have you done any computer programming?"

I shake my head.

"Any electronics?"

"Not really."

"Any summer camps in gaming?"

I sigh. Obviously, I have a lot to learn.

"Think about the fifth-grade class." Ms. Freeman puts on a polite smile and turns back to her students.

From across the room, I hear Red Shirt shout, "Yes! This end effector is going to be way better than the net!"

End effector? Okay, maybe this class would be too much for me. But fifth graders? Maybe staying in soccer is okay after all.

As I stand in the swirl of possibilities, I'm startled to see the nurse striding toward me in light yellow scrubs. "There you are! Coach radioed that you were coming to see me."

"I, um . . ."

"Come on, let's make sure you're okay before your next class."

I let her guide me down the hall, but pictures of robots and Ping-Pong balls scroll in my head. I think over what Ms. Freeman said. Intro class, Robotics 1, Robotics 2. I'm a radio whose dial is turning, turning, trying to tune in to a signal.

I never thought of myself as a computer geek. There aren't many techy types on the soccer team. But geeky or not, robotics looks fun, and today's soccer sure wasn't.

Maybe the fifth-grade intro class wouldn't be so bad? But what about next year? I'd move up along with my "little friends." I need to find a way to take Robotics 2 with kids in my own grade.

The dial in my brain keeps turning, but I'm still hearing static.

After school, I drop my backpack in the hall and walk into the dining room on the way to a snack, still thinking of R2-D2 and Ms. Freeman's robotics room.

Dad's studying a landscape plan spread out across the table. I recognize the green graph lines. He's deep in concentration but says "Hey" as he pencils a note.

I take a closer look. Little circles show where he'll plant bushes, and bigger circles show trees. Since he's the boss of Véliz Verde, he plans where to put grass, patios, and even fountains for hotels.

X-ing out a line of bushes, he says, "Your mom's at rehearsal."

During the spring concert season, Mom rehearses a lot. She leads all three student bands at her school.

Dad talks to the paper. "I thought I'd make pizza. An early supper?"

I can't help remembering how just a few months ago, this table was where he showed me soccer strategies. He'd make a circle for each position—fullback, wingback, forward, striker—and then draw arrows to show me different plays.

"Dad? Have you ever used a robot?"

"A robot?" He looks up, his eyes tired. "We have that Roomba somewhere."

"Oh, yeah." I hadn't thought of our little round vacuum cleaner as a robot. "Well, wouldn't it be cool to learn how to make them? Like, program them and stuff?"

"Sure, yeah." I get the feeling he's not really listening, because he's looking back at his landscape plan.

"They have some robots at school. I saw them today."

"That's great, Luz." He writes something down.

Should I tell him about the intro class? I'm not sure he'll be happy about it. It means dropping out of soccer.

I try again. "Robots run by following computer programs."

"Yup. As long as they don't put me out of a job." He sighs as he says this, his chest deflating. "How about that pizza?" he asks.

Wow. I wasn't expecting him to jump up and down, but I never heard anyone less interested in robots. As he goes to the kitchen, I sit at the dining table. I scratch at a dot of dried milk with my thumbnail. Maybe I can program something so cool that he *will* be interested. Like a game or an app or a simulation of how stars are born. Or maybe he only gets excited about fútbol.

"Want to watch the match this weekend?" I ask. "It's a qualifying game."

"I don't know," he says, opening the oven door. I wish he'd grab the remote and find a game for us on TV right now.

"Or tonight?" With all the sports channels, there's always a match going on somewhere in the world. "We can criticize their attack patterns."

His smile flares and then fades. "How's the leg?"

"It's fine."

"You're not twisting it, are you?" Now he looks at me directly. Is that the only thing he can talk to me about?

"No. It's great, Dad."

He nods and pulls plates out of the cupboard. "Sorry, Luz. I'll be meeting with a client on Saturday. Big landscaping job. No time for a game tonight."

There's never time anymore. Why not? He's the boss, and his workers do the actual planting. When he started, he did it all himself and still found time to date Mom. The story goes that the first house she rented sat on a red desert of rock and clay. The landlord found a specialist who would design a landscape that used very little water—my dad. Mom was so impressed that she asked more questions than he had time to answer, so they went to dinner.

Is he against everything soccer now? It feels like he's against *me*. And why don't we joke around anymore? Does he think I'm too old or something?

Soon a plate sits in front of me. The melted cheese looks like old chewing gum stretched over the dough. I can't say I'm hungry.

After supper, I trudge to my room with the last of some math homework. Zigzag leaps to the windowsill to watch birds swooping, and I wonder if Mr. Mac could invent a wider shelfy thing for her to sit on. I don't know how he'd attach it to the window, but he's practically a genius, so— then the radio dial in my head, the one that was turning, turning, turning at school, locks on to a signal.

Learning Robotics 1 without taking the class. How to attend computer-gaming-electronics camp without going anywhere. My brain goes from pulses of static to a clear, loud idea. Mr. Mac! He could teach me.

But will he want to do it? He's doing that project for his grandson. . . . But he's Gadget Santa, right? Grandpa of the neighborhood, who built himself a mailbox sensor and then made one for us, too? (Now we get a text message when there's mail in there, plus a little green light on the box goes on.) I bet he would do it. And I could still stay in Athletic Hour.

A rhyme from elementary school flits through my mind. *Crossing fingers, crossing toes; hope for yesses, not for no's!*

I check the time. Could I ask him right now? I rub Zigzag under her chin, and she seems to be saying, "Why not?"

"You're right," I tell her. "Dad, I'm going to Mr. Mac's!" I slip my jacket on and head across the street.

I step onto the smooth concrete floor of the garage. "Mr. Mac?"

He looks up from the workbench and smiles, his cheeks almost touching his round glasses. "Great to see you, Luz. I was just sanding this wood."

A stiff piece of sandpaper crinkles in his hand, and a woodsy smell meets my nose. I'm excited to ask him to teach me everything he knows about computers, but I need to wait for a good opening.

"See these lines in the wood?" he says. "That's the grain. Always sand with the grain, not across it."

He hands me a square of sandpaper. At first it slips across the wood, but I press harder until a fine cloud of wood dust poofs up. "What's it for?" I ask.

"I'm making a wrist rest. So my hands are more comfortable while typing. My hands have been kind of . . ." He holds them straight out, and I see that they tremble some. "Well, never mind. What's up?"

"Mmm." I bite my bottom lip, trying to think of how to ask what I'm thinking of asking. "So, there's this class."

He sets aside his wrist rest and lowers himself into his swiveling desk chair. He props his chin on his cane. "A class at school. Okay. Go on."

"I want to take Robotics Two next year. They're building robots in there!"

"Sounds good." He sticks his head forward as if waiting for me to say something more. "But?"

"But I'm supposed to take two other classes first. A semester of Intro and a semester of Robotics One." Mr. Mac doesn't look shocked enough. I lock my eyes right on his. "That means waiting a whole year before I can build robots like I saw today. One of them scoops up Ping-Pong balls."

"Impressive! I'm glad your school has that class. You could probably learn a lot from those first two courses, though." When he sees my frown, he goes on. "Have you asked the teacher to bend the rules?"

"She says I have to take the intro class with fifth graders if I want to learn anything this year. But that still doesn't get me into Robotics Two by next fall." I realize that I'm grumbling now. I hear my mom's voice in my head. *Don't pout! Don't roll your eyes! Not if you want people to listen.* That always makes me want to pout more. *And* roll my eyes.

"The intro class will let you start at least, which—"

I interrupt him with a sigh. "That's what Ms. Freeman said. I could go into the fifth-grade class for now, but I don't want to be stuck with the little kids forever. Do you think I could . . . that is, I was wondering . . . like, maybe if I could get ahead. You know . . ." I scan the room.

"You want to learn outside of the class?" He looks over his glasses at me, and our eyes meet. "But you're not sure how to do it?"

I put on my most hopeful smile. "Unless . . ."

Mr. Mac slaps his knee. "Of course I'll help you! We can start right now." His voice drops lower as he talks more to himself than to me. "We'll have to show the teacher what you've learned somehow. We could always send her a file . . . she might have a test for you . . . Say!" He meets my eyes. "When do you have to be home for supper?"

I'm still processing that this means yes. "Oh, thank you, Mr. Mac! This is amazing! I can't tell you—"

"Happy to help. Supper is when?"

"I already ate."

"Excellent!" He springs up and starts gathering supplies. He opens drawers and cabinets and drops a pile of parts on his workbench in the middle of the garage. I didn't know he could move in high gear like this. Not even his cane slows him down.

"Pull up a stool," he says.

We each take a stool and scoot it up to the workbench. "I could ask the teacher for the textbook," I say, trying to sound helpful.

"No, no." He bats the air with his hand. "Kiddo, I'm pretty sure I've written program documentation more complicated than any book they're using."

Documentation? Maybe that's like instructions or something.

"I hate to say it, Luz, but some of these textbooks are all hat and no cattle."

I suppose he's right, but a twinge of worry pinches me. This *is* exactly what I'd hoped for, but does he know what robotics class covers? I mean, he definitely knows a lot. He's, like, Einstein meets Sherlock Holmes. I just hope he teaches me what I need to learn.

"Robots take their instructions from a computer, so let's start there. Have you ever heard of binary?"

I shake my head, but the "bi" part sounds familiar. "Is it two of something?"

"Right-ee-o! *Bi*nary. *Bi*cycle. *Bi*noculars. Two. In this case it refers to the basis of all computer languages. Zero and one."

Oh, man. This sounds like not just the ground floor of programming, but the prehistoric ruins under the foundations.

I must look a little freaked out, because Mr. Mac chuckles. "Don't worry, Luz. I won't make you talk to a computer in zeros and ones, but I want to show you something. You need to know how a computer thinks. And that begins . . . here."

He hands me a tiny light bulb.

I chuckle under my breath because my name means "light." It's just a coincidence, but I think Mr. Mac picked a good place to start.

"Twist that light bulb into the little holder there."
Mr. Mac points to where I should put the mini light bulb.

The "holder" looks like a doll's top hat with a hole in the
middle. I screw the bulb in.

"Now attach this." He hands me a wire. "See the metal
end?" he says. "I've stripped off some of the plastic coating."

Sure enough, I can attach the wire to the holder. It has
a screw on either side. I slide the wire under one screw and
tighten it with a tiny screwdriver that Mr. Mac hands me at
just the right moment.

I do the same with a second wire.

The wires look like hairs sticking out of the doll hat, one
on each side.

"Connect one wire to the battery. Connect the other
one to this switch." He points out what connects to what,
but he lets me do each step. "Here's the last wire."

Soon we have a wire circle that connects all the parts—
bulb holder, battery, and switch.

"Try it out," he says, nodding at the switch.

I flip the switch, and the light blazes, the little filament inside glowing for all its worth. A part of me lights up, too.

I flip the switch. Off. On. Off. On.

"This is how a computer thinks."

I had forgotten all about computers.

"A silicon chip has millions of tiny switches. Each bit of information is a yes or a no, a one or a zero, an on or an off. Binary."

"But how can it mean anything?" My mind is slightly blown that my switch is anything like a computer chip.

"Patterns. Anything that can be represented with electrical patterns," he says, "can be represented in patterns of bits—patterns of zeros and ones. The computer's memory stores the bit patterns, all the ons and offs."

I'm quiet, trying to absorb this.

"You've also built a nice circuit there." Mr. Mac gestures with his chin. "That was your first lesson in both electronics and programming."

My chest expands, and I stand up straighter. Hope fills up the crowded garage. I can do this. *We* can do this. If I learn from Mr. Mac for nine weeks and then all summer, I'll be more than ready for Robotics 2, won't I?

"You best get on home," Mr. Mac says gently. "It's getting dark. I'll work on a plan for next time."

"Can't we do some more right now?" I'm ready to turn on a computer and learn a command or whatever.

"I love your energy, Luz, but let me give this some thought. 'To make an apple pie, you must first invent the universe,' you know?"

"What?"

"Carl Sagan. The astronomer? That's him right there." He points to one of the posters. "It's a quote. It means that a vast preparation came before we could exist. Possibly four-point-six billion years. But I won't need that long." He winks. "Give me a day to gather our supplies. When I worked at Texas Instruments, I was just like you—ready to get going, and busier than a one-armed coat hanger!"

"What's Texas Instruments?" I ask.

"A technology company. They had an old computer over there that was as big as this garage."

"Whoa. Were the switches big?"

"As big as that mini light bulb and not too different. Vacuum tubes, they're called. Thousands of little bulbs can take up some space, I'll tell you! They also make a bunch of heat, so we needed coolers, too."

Now I see why computers were so big. I always wondered about that.

My mind rewinds to Ms. Freeman and the intro class. "Hey, Mr. Mac? If we do this every day . . . you know, learning stuff? Do you think I can skip that intro class? It's not just the fifth graders." I swallow. "I'd also have to drop soccer. They're both first period."

Mr. Mac pushes up his glasses and strokes his chin. "Well now, that's a tough decision."

The air has turned cooler with the sun riding the edge of the horizon. A little heater in the corner clicks on.

"You know what I always say?" Mr. Mac gestures to his tool board. "A self is not discovered, but created."

I meet his eyes, trying to understand his meaning.

"You can build yourself. Create who you want to be. Soccer is part of you—your history, your store of knowledge. Do you want to add something new? Look at my wrist rest there. I thought I'd use wood. Simple pine. Now I think I'll add a layer of foam. Make it more comfortable. You can add layers, too, to your life. But it's not a requirement. Sure, you'll learn plenty here, and maybe soccer class is fun." He looks at me intently. "Like I said, you have a tough choice."

Soccer class wasn't fun today. I flip my switch on and off again. *This* was fun. I want to add this to my build-a-Luz for sure.

"Thanks, Mr. Mac. That Intro to Robotics class is looking better than I thought." I look around at the workbench, the tools, the computers. Everything sorted, everything ready to be used. Maybe it's true. *A self is not discovered, but created.* I don't want to leave, but I force myself to say goodbye.

"I'll look for you tomorrow." Mr. Mac waves.

Crossing the street, I feel more sure with each step. In a whole summer, I can learn a lot, but Intro *would* be a good start. And in August when school begins, I'll need a way to prove everything to Ms. Freeman, of course. Maybe turn on a computer and show her? Or email my code, whatever that is? Tomorrow, I'll stop by her room and tell her my garage-school plan. I'll learn so much, she'll have to let me in Robotics 2.

A zipping sound pulls me out of my thoughts, and Little Red shoots around my legs, bumping the curb. The tray holds my switch! I lift it out and turn to Mr. Mac.

"You can keep that," he calls.

"Thanks!" I wave.

As I climb the driveway, I'm greeted by the dining room light shining out over the dark yard.

My high spirits lower as soon as I step in the house. "It's not like I planned this!" Dad says. It's not quite a yell, but it's angry.

"I know!" says Mom, just as emphatically. "I'm just asking how we should—Luz, is that you?"

"Yes," I say.

They go quiet, and I know they've decided to not fight in front of me. But it's not like I can't tell that the mood of the house is all slantwise. Tilty, off-kilter, cattywampus. And it's not just angry words. Mom seems sad, and Dad works too much. I think it started with The Leg. It made Mom and Dad disagree about surgery. And I haven't given them anything new to cheer about.

Maybe this new plan of Luz the Computer Whiz will bring some cheering back.

I'm on a mission this morning. I'm going to ask Ms. Martin to move me into the fifth-grade Intro to Robotics class. I pull open the heavy double doors at school as soon as they're unlocked.

But in the front office, I stop cold.

Skyler and another team member, Marissa, stand at the desk in their practice jerseys. Skyler's got a soccer ball propped on her hip, her arm draping over it.

"I need to call my mom," she's saying to Mr. Wilson, the assistant who basically runs the whole school from his perfectly organized desk. "I need her to bring me my lunch."

"I understand, Skyler. You can use this phone after I make one more call. We're needing a substitute teacher in biology today." Mr. Wilson is already pressing the numbers on the phone.

"This is why we need cell phones, right?" Skyler says to Marissa.

"Totally," Marissa says.

I'm surprised to see them off the field. Practice usually starts before school.

"Oh, it's Luz." Skyler gestures "hey" with her chin. "Are you coming to first period?"

My routine has been to join them at 8:30. And seeing their outfits and cleated shoes, seeing the soccer ball with its scuffs and grass stains, smelling the leather—it almost makes me want to walk right out there with them. But then I think of the bench—the boring, butt-warm bench.

"Luz?" Marissa catches my eye.

"Uh, yeah. I'll be there today at least."

"What do you mean?" Skyler says, switching the ball to her other hip.

"Well . . ." Suddenly I'm not sure about getting out. In soccer, at least they remember who I was, what I was. Last season's high-scorer.

"Guess who's playing your position today." Marissa's voice is soaked with annoyance. "Lacie! Can you believe it? She can't be the striker!"

"Lacie *can* run," I say. "But all month it's been that eighth grader."

"So why the change, right? I don't know. Just giving Lacie a chance, maybe?" Skyler shrugs. "I'm happy to be a defender."

"Same, same," Marissa assures her. She leans into Skyler until their arms look Velcroed together. I remember doing that with Veronica from soccer camp, but she goes to another school. And Skyler used to kid around with me, but we weren't Velcro-close. I guess I've never had a true BFF. It occurs to me that I won't know *anyone* if I switch classes.

"So what are you doing here?" Marissa's eyes fasten on mine.

"Uh, the nurse. My knee's acting up today." The lie slips out before I can think.

"That's too bad," Skyler says. "You going to Mama's Pizza after the game on Friday?"

"I haven't been to the last six games, Sky. Ever since . . ."

"Yeah, I know, but you could still come for pizza. We miss you."

I want this to be true. It *could* be. But this is the first time anyone's mentioned my coming out with the team since the accident. They did send a card. Skyler's signature was the biggest, surrounded by a bunch of hearts and smiley faces.

"Your mom can call mine if you need a ride," she says.

"Wow, that's really nice." I feel bad saying no. "I'll think about it."

"Sounds like a 'no' to me." Skyler looks at Marissa.

"Sure does." Marissa cocks an eyebrow back.

"Whatever you want." Skyler turns to Mr. Wilson. "*Now* can I call my mom?"

"Here you go," he says, swiveling the phone to face her.

As she dials, I remember that I told them I was going to the nurse. But something nags at me. Skyler doesn't understand, and I want her to know that I'm not shutting out the team. When she hangs up, I follow them out of the office.

"Hey, Sky? It's not that I don't miss the games."

She listens.

"It's just that . . . well, seeing everyone else play makes me sad. And Mama's Pizza, it's a replay, right? Who scored and who assisted and everything."

The after-game is all about reliving the game. The game I didn't play.

Skyler points her gaze down the row of lockers. "Yeah, but, you know, Luz, you could just cheer for us."

A coldness falls through my body.

Is she right? Should I be going to the games? I flip between feeling hurt and feeling guilty. Maybe I should be supporting the team. Maybe I'm jealous of their healthy knees. Or maybe it's just this: If I sit in the stands, I'm no use to anyone. Not running + not executing a play = not special. I have no reason to be there.

I decide to tell them my news. "The thing is, I might, uh, get out of soccer."

Both of them stare at me.

I might as well go on. "Since I can't play, I'm thinking I'll switch to some other class."

Skyler takes a step toward me, and her expression softens. "But you love the game. And you've always been in soccer."

"I know." I look at the floor, feeling the heavy truth of it.

"And your dad was *so* into it. I never saw a parent coach be so, I don't know, professional about it. The League team hasn't been the same since Ms. Hanson took over."

Now I feel even worse. Not only have I let down my school team, but Dad's let down the League team. All because of me.

"I'm sorry."

"Luz, it's okay," says Marissa. "Everyone knows your dad wouldn't want to coach after what happened."

Skyler nods in agreement.

"Thanks."

"We'd miss you in soccer class, you know," Skyler says.

I look away. If this week's taught me anything, it's that no one truly thinks about me during class. And really, they shouldn't. They should focus on their skills and learning the best moves to beat a defender. "I don't think anyone will notice much, Sky."

Marissa stays quiet. She probably agrees with me.

"Well, of course we're busy playing, but I mean . . ." She struggles to make her point. "I'm used to you being there."

This is a weak argument, and she knows it.

"It's just so sad that you got hurt," she adds.

"Yeah." I never know what to say when people say that. Pity was okay at first, but now it's getting old. It doesn't help me.

"Can't you bring out the water and the towels and stuff?"

"I could do that, but it's not the same."

She bobs her head, and I think she's seeing it the way I do now.

"Hey, we better get back to the field," Marissa says. "See you around, Luz."

Skyler's eyes linger on mine. I help her go. "See y'all soon," I say.

With a final wave, she and Marissa drop the ball and pass it back and forth down the hall toward the doors that lead to the field.

I stride back to the office, more certain than ever. In soccer, I'm not the star, not even the crutches kid. Just invisible. Who cares about the water girl? Even Skyler gets it now.

It's time to get into Robotics.

The school counselor, Ms. Martin, gets the okay from Mom and Dad, and it's official. I'm enrolled in Introduction to Robotics. "Monday morning you'll go to Mr. Sung's class across the street at the elementary school," she says.

Though everything is the same—Ms. Martin's Kleenex box that looks like a head with tissue coming out its nose, the cougar mascot painted on the wall—I feel like I've stepped off a bus in a new town. Robotics Town, I guess.

"You know where to go Monday?" Ms. Martin asks.

"Yeah, thanks."

I can find C-24, no problem. I know that whole school like I know the size of a soccer field. But I've never met Mr. Sung, and when I try to picture what we'll do in his class, my brain is an empty whiteboard. I guess I'll find out soon enough.

Now I have to convince Ms. Freeman of my garage-schooling plan. All day, I think about what to say. I try out different phrases, then change them around, like Dad rearranging plants to make the right impression. I have to make skipping a semester of Robotics sound reasonable. She has to think of spring and summer with Mr. Mac like camp at Apple's headquarters.

After school, I pat R2-D2 on his domed head and cross Ms. Freeman's threshold. Immediately, I note the red-shirt boy working in the corner. That kid likes red. And he loves robotics so much that he comes after school.

"I remember you," Ms. Freeman says, walking over from a computer. "Did you think about that intro class?"

"Yes ma'am." In Texas, it's always good to throw in a ma'am to be polite. "I just changed my schedule. I'll start Monday."

"That's great, Miss—?"

"Véliz. Luz Véliz."

"Great to hear it, Luz." She turns to leave, her boldly colored full skirt whooshing.

"There's one more thing, Ms. Freeman. I have a . . . a proposition." Mom uses this word when she announces a new plan.

Ms. Freeman tilts her head like she's interested, or maybe a little surprised. She leans against her desk, and I start explaining. I tell her about Mr. MacLellan, building my first circuit, and how I think I can learn a lot between now and next fall.

"I'm impressed, Luz," she says. "This Mr. MacLellan sounds like a great resource. We should bring him in as a guest speaker."

I find myself rising up on my toes. This is going great.

"Here's the thing, though."

Oh, no.

"I have limited spots in that R-Two class. If it fills up at the end of the year, I won't have a place to offer you. Let me explain. Have you heard of the May Showcase?"

I'm listening carefully. "Is that the science fair at the end of school?"

"It does include science projects, but it's also where Robotics One students show their computer programs. Some students showcase actual robots; others demonstrate their code, often a game. I select the most promising students to go into Robotics Two."

"What about everyone else?" I blurt out.

"We have a robotics club that's open to everyone. The school doesn't have enough computers and supplies for everyone to take the class."

"So I'll need to present something in the Showcase?"

She looks startled. "Well, yes, if you want to try for a spot in the class. But Luz, I want to be honest with you. You'll be competing against students who have spent a long time learning their code and working on their projects. The Showcase is the last Friday night of the school year. You only have nine weeks."

Nine weeks. Not all summer. For a moment, I feel a weight pulling me down. My body wants to sink through the floor.

Then I remember how I got good at scoring in soccer. I practiced in the heat and the cold. I wore out two leather balls practicing my footwork and my aim. I asked a lot of questions. I watched great players. Then I picture my parents, happy and linking arms to cheer me on. I want to see that again, and not a year from now.

"Ms. Freeman, I know nine weeks isn't much, but I can do it." I don't know if I sound confident or just desperate.

"Luz, I appreciate your—"

"I can at least try, right?"

She doesn't say no.

"If I write a program, will you let me demonstrate it at the Showcase?"

She shakes her head, then opens her mouth and closes it. She looks into space, then brings her eyes level with mine. "I can give you a slot in the list of presenters and a computer. It's up to you to bring your code on a flash drive."

"Yes ma'am." I'm afraid to let my excitement show too much—*What if she changes her mind?*—but my heart is racing.

"And remember, if you don't make that class, you can still take Robotics One."

"I know, Ms. Freeman. The thing is, I mean . . . that would mean being with the younger kids *again*."

"Is that so important?"

"Maybe not." *At least it wouldn't be across at the elementary school.* "But I'll do it, Ms. Freeman. I'll show you I can." Another thought strikes me. "Can parents come to the Showcase?"

"Sure, they can. I encourage all students to bring someone. We get parents, grandparents, aunts, uncles . . ."

I wonder if Mom and Dad would come. I picture them dressing up, Dad in a suit and Mom in heels. Dad would slick his hair back and put his hand on my shoulder, like he used to when I won a trophy.

Ms. Freeman smiles like she's actually happy with me. "Good luck, Luz. And hey, check out the robotics club. It meets Fridays after school."

The same as game night. But that doesn't matter, does it? Nope, nope, nope. That was before, before, before. "Thanks. I'll come."

The red-shirt boy watches me from a worktable across the room. I imagine what Skyler would think of him. *Looks a little nerdy, doesn't he?* He does, with the glasses and the skinny jeans, but something about his mop of curly hair and rich brown skin makes my eyes want to keep looking.

Ms. Freeman stands, and I bring my gaze back to her. "This is the room," she says. "For the club. Four to five p.m."

"Thanks, Ms. Freeman."

As I leave, I stop and pat R2-D2 again. His red light shines like a smile. "Wouldn't Mr. Mac love you?" I say to him. "He could probably program you to fly a plane or something."

I hope Mr. Mac's ready to teach me everything he can—and fast.

When I rush into Mr. Mac's garage after school, he's already typing at a computer. Surprisingly, it's got a flat screen. That must be the newest thing in here.

"Mr. Mac! I'm going to be in that class, Intro to Robotics. I start Monday!"

"Luz!" He swivels to face me. "Nice to see you! That's excellent."

"But we don't have as much time as I thought. I have to finish a project for a Showcase in nine weeks!"

"Ooo-wee. That's coming right up."

"Is that enough time? Can you teach me that fast?"

"We'll do our best. Starting right now. Come see what I'm working on."

I drop my backpack and look over his shoulder at the screen. "What's this?"

"I told you about that project for my grandson, right?"

Symbols and text fill the screen. Indents, like at the beginning of a paragraph, must be important, because almost every line is indented farther than the one before.

Mr. Mac types a few more lines and clicks SAVE. "Let me show you the general layout of this." He scrolls up through screen after screen, until it resembles a waterfall. "Don't worry about what the code actually says. Look at the sections. See this chunk? All the lines are indented the same amount. That means these lines are one team, accomplishing one process."

It looks like a paragraph, basically. "What happens here?" I point to a place where the line outdents.

"That line matches this one farther up. *They* are on the same team. And if we scroll around, you can see that the entire program is teams within teams. In fact, we can draw a map of this program on paper."

The waterfall turns out to be very organized.

"Hand me a sheet from the printer, would you?"

He draws a diamond at the top. "This program takes in a signal. Depending on what type it is, it skips to different commands."

I'm listening, but I'm not sure I'm following. "So . . ." I'm not sure what I need to ask.

"Come sit so you can see."

I pull up a stool as he writes "SIGNAL" in the diamond at the top of the page.

"First, the signal comes in. Then . . ."—he draws a line down from the diamond and makes a rectangle—"the program has to decide if it's type A or B or C or whatever. Which team it's on." He writes "DETERMINE SIGNAL."

Then he draws three arms that end in squares labeled A, B, and C.

"Once the computer knows which type of signal it is, it can hop down to the right command." Now he draws more shapes, connecting each one back to the A, B, C squares.

"This looks scary complicated," I say.

Mr. Mac laughs. "You know what Marie Curie would say to that?" He takes a second to point her out on the wall. "'Nothing is to be feared, it is only to be understood. Now is the time to understand more, so that we may fear less.'" He raises his eyebrows as if to ask if I understand. "I know it looks complicated, Luz, but a flowchart like this makes coding easier. Once I have my map, I can code each part and know that all the sections will work together."

That makes sense. "Wait, what does this program even do?"

"Oh! I should have started with that." Mr. Mac takes off his glasses and wipes them with a cloth. "This program interprets a homing signal sent to the computer." He must see that my eyes are still squinting, trying to grasp what that means. "It's a tracking device."

"Like, for finding your keys?"

"Similar. But most trackers depend on satellites. I'm using something older: radio."

"Is that better?"

Mr. Mac sits back in his chair. "In some ways. My tracker is very small, and its battery lasts for months without charging."

"Are you going sell a bunch of them and get rich?"

Mr. Mac laughs. "No, I'm only making a few."

"Just for fun? But it's so much work." It's cool and all, but it looks more like a job than a hobby. And it definitely doesn't seem like a toy for a kid.

Mr. Mac searches the ceiling for a moment, then puts on his glasses. "Have you heard of autism, Luz?"

"Yes. Two kids in my class have it."

"My grandson has it. Connor. A little older than you. He's a smart boy, but he doesn't always recognize danger. And he doesn't answer questions fast; he needs extra time. Recently, he started leaving the house."

"Leaving? You mean, he just walks out by himself?"

"It's more like wandering. His parents keep having to look for him. And he doesn't know where all the streets go. Last time, the police brought him home."

I imagine how sick with worry my parents would be if I were missing. I trace the wood-grain pattern on the workbench with my fingertip. "So you're making this for him. To track him, so he won't get lost." It's sinking in that Mr. Mac isn't just my neighbor, my tutor, Grandpa of the neighborhood. To Connor, he's a real, actual grandpa. A good one.

"Yes, so we can find him when he wanders."

"When will you finish?"

"A few more weeks should do it."

It occurs to me that Mr. Mac might not have time to teach me, with such an urgent project on hand. My voice comes out very quiet. "Mr. Mac, this is important."

"Yes, it is. But I still have time to teach you, if that's worrying you."

I let out a nervous laugh. "That *is* worrying me."

"No need, no need. I usually work on this in the mornings. I race the sun to my saddle, as they say."

This explains why I see a light on in his garage when I leave for school.

"Let's turn on a different computer." Mr. Mac claps and rubs his hands together. "Are you ready to write your first program?"

"I sure am!" I wonder which computer I'll work on.

Before Mr. Mac can slide off his stool, a voice wavers through the air from outside. "Hola, Mr. MacLellan." It's Dad. I didn't hear him coming. I wonder why he's here.

"Mr. Véliz. ¡Bienvenido! Luz and I were just about to start her first real program."

"I'm sorry to interrupt." Dad doesn't step into the garage, but stands a foot away. He's usually more of a right-up-close person. Warm. Jokey. But not now.

"Quite all right." Mr. Mac smiles, but he seems to be waiting.

An uncomfortable silence falls over the three of us.

I hop off my stool. "What is it, Dad?"

"We, um, got a phone call." Dad looks from me to Mr. Mac and back again. "We've had news from Guatemala."

"Sounds important," Mr. Mac says.

My father's face, I notice now, is paler than I've ever seen.

I step forward, thinking of my Guatemalan abuelos, the grandparents I've only met a few times. "Has Abuelito died? Abuelita?"

"Your abuelos are fine, mija."

Dad says "my daughter" in Spanish when he's trying to be tender, when he's trying to soften a blow.

"There's something else . . . " he says, staring at a point beyond my head.

"I guess I better go," I say to Mr. Mac, grabbing my backpack.

"I hope everything is okay." Mr. Mac says it almost like a question.

Dad looks lost, as if he hasn't heard anything, but he answers quietly. "Our life here—your life, Luz—is about to change forever."

12

"Sit down, Luz," Dad says.

We're at the dining room table again. At least it's not about me this time. *Or is it?*

"Did school go okay?" Mom asks, as if this is a normal moment. She shoves a stack of music to the empty end of the table.

"Yeah, I switched into Robotics, the intro class, remember?" No one says anything. "But what's this about?" Dad said my abuelos didn't die. What else could it be?

"I made chili," Dad announces. He grates cheddar cheese over each steaming bowl. "Cornbread, too!"

This is getting weird. Why is he trying to turn dinner into some kind of special occasion? I watch him closely.

After setting the cornbread in the middle of the table, he doesn't sit, but fidgets, shifting his weight from one foot to the other.

"Honey." Mom gives him a sad smile. "It's going to be all right."

"What is?" I burst out. "What's going on?"

Dad sits down at last. He moves to push up his glasses, but he still has oven mitts on, so he ends up patting his nose. He laughs nervously, lays the mitts aside, and faces me. "Luz, we're going to have a visitor."

"Not a visitor, Emilio," Mom says quietly.

"Right. Of course. No. Not a visitor." He tries again. "We're going to have a child, a girl . . ."

"A baby?" I never expected this. Mom and Dad tried to get pregnant years ago, but I hadn't heard them talk about it recently.

"No, not a baby." Dad drops his head in his hands. "¡A la gran—!" He's running out of patience with himself, but I'm still lost.

"Luz," Mom starts, "in Guatemala, there's—"

"No, I should say it." Dad takes a deep breath. "I have a daughter."

I blink. Of course he has a daughter. I'm his daughter.

Dad sees that I don't understand because he leans forward and speaks slowly. "I have a daughter in Guatemala."

"What?"

"Her name is Solana," he says.

The words sit like the shreds of cheese on top of my chili, not sinking in.

"She's thirteen."

Older than me? I do some math in my head. I'm eleven. She must have been born just before my parents got married. How did we never hear of her? I find my voice. "How did this happen?"

"Well." Dad halts, and his face reddens by two shades.

"No, I mean . . . like, why didn't we see her on our trip to Guatemala? Why haven't I met her? You're not her mom?" I look at Mom as I say this, almost wishing I hadn't asked. Something else occurs to me. "How do you know she's really . . . you know, *yours*?"

"I had the same questions, Luz," Mom says. "Believe me."

I bet she did. In fact, lots of stuff makes sense now. The lowered voices. The strained faces. Those sharp conversations behind their bedroom door. I thought Mom and Dad were angry at each other or angry with me. This must be what they've been working through.

Mom says, "They've done a DNA test, and it's true. Solana is your father's child."

Dad's eyes meet mine, and I read an apology there. "I didn't know about her, myself, Luz. Her mother and I . . ." He swallows and clears his throat. "We met about a year before I met your mother. When we broke up, I didn't know she was pregnant. I never saw her again, and she never told me. She raised Solana on her own."

I don't know what to feel. My heart panics to think of Dad with another woman. But then, that same heart is melting for this girl who grew up without a dad. Or at least, without my dad. Or, I guess I should say, without *our* dad?

"Sweetheart," Mom says steadily, "we would have told you sooner, but we wanted to be sure. I wanted to be sure." She says this last part to herself.

"Do you have a picture or something?" I suddenly want to know more, more, more. Who is this person who is half similar to me? What is her life like?

Dad taps his phone and brings up a photo.

A thud lands in my stomach. She's beautiful. The picture must have been taken at church or a dance or a wedding or something. Her long, dark hair lies thick on her shoulders. My own hair is plain brown, kind of like sunflower seeds, not that deep walnut like hers. Her white dress falls just to the knee, its style more full and flouncy than any dress I've ever had. Something about her jaw reminds me of Dad. Something about her forehead reminds me of me.

"Lucita." Dad takes his phone back and looks into my eyes. "Mija. There's more."

"Another daughter?"

Dad almost laughs.

"Don't even joke about that," Mom says with a wan smile.

Dad looks at the ceiling, as if the right words are floating up there. "Solana's . . . well, she's been through a tough time. Last year, her mother died."

"Oh. That's . . ." Now it's my turn to struggle for words. I was going to say "sad," but whatever it feels like to lose a mom, that word runs circles around "sad."

"She's been living with her aunt," Mom says.

"But that was temporary." Dad squares his shoulders. "She can't live there anymore. They have four kids already. Staying there gave us time to sort things out, get paperwork signed. The embassy finally called today. Solana's coming next week."

I must look stunned because Mom fills in the silence. "Coming here to live, Luz. To live with us."

Suddenly the room feels too small. The table seems to tip. "No!" I shout. "She can't live with us. We've never even met her before."

"I've done video calls with her, Luz. You'll like her. I know it," Dad says.

"You've been video-calling her? When was this?" Somehow I feel betrayed, like he should have video-called me, too. I know this makes no sense, but I'm still jealous. Besides, they're doing this all wrong. They should let us get to know each other, like just weekends at first. Take us on a road trip, maybe. This is not how they do it in movies about adoption or divorced people blending their families or whatever. This is not right.

Dad sits back, his face sagging. "I hoped you might . . . be a little happy."

"Happy? Happy that I'm about to share my house with a stranger?" My voice rises, and I know I shouldn't be shouting. I've never truly yelled at my parents before, not since I was little anyway.

"Luz." My mother's voice is firm. "She's lost her mom. She's lost her home. She's about to leave her country. *We* are her family."

"What about the aunt? She's family, too."

"There are good reasons, Luz, trust me. Besides, I'm her father. She's my responsibility." Dad is sitting up straighter now.

"Why? Has she even met you? No. Did you raise her? No. Does she know anything about you? Nothing!"

I've only seen my dad cry once before. It was in November, when I was loaded into the ambulance. Now I see wetness in the corners of his eyes.

"We'll never love you less, Luz," Mom says. "No one can take your place. But you have a sister. A sister who needs us. Who needs you."

Tears roll down my cheeks, and I'm not sure if I'm crying for Solana or for myself or for the whole mess. Dad moves toward me, but I stand up and back away.

"Tell her to stay there. Tell her not to come!" I'm crying for real now, sobbing and snotty.

Dad steps toward me again. Great, after he's avoided me for months.

I run toward my room, and of course now, of all times, my knee gives way. I crash to the floor, but I push myself up, ignoring the pain in my ankle and the carpet burn on the heels of my hands, ignoring the bruise that's probably forming on my knee. Ignoring my parents calling my name.

I huff through school, limping a little. Nothing in the day turns off the *no, no, no* in my head and the terrible feeling that I've been downgraded. Demoted from soccer star to kid sister.

I skip Mr. Mac's after school and trudge home. I flop onto the couch, and Zigzag jumps up beside me. I half hope that Solana is allergic to cats.

I startle when a key turns in the front door lock, and the door opens. "Luz, are you here?" Mom calls from the entryway.

"I'm here!" I shout. I guess she's not rehearsing late.

"Oh, good." Mom sets down two cloth bags and her jacket. "I don't know why I assign those History of Music essays. Now I have to grade them." She pours herself some sweet iced tea. "Want some?"

"No thanks," I say from the couch. It's warming up outside, but I'm still in hot chocolate mode.

Mom sighs into the puffy chair across from me. "Was school good? You started that new class, right?"

"That's Monday."

"Oh. Well, did anything interesting happen?"

"Getting a new sister is interesting enough."

She takes a deep breath and releases it before talking. "I know it's going to be hard, Luz. Having Solana here. I never expected anything like this either." She stares at her tea.

"We don't even know her."

"True."

For a moment, I feel heard. Mom and I both got a surprise. I guess Dad did, too, actually.

"But we will." She finally takes a sip.

"I guess."

"I only wish we'd taught you Spanish."

"Wait, what?" I sit upright.

"She's Guatemalan, Luz. She speaks Spanish."

"Well, yeah, but . . . You mean, *only* Spanish? She doesn't know English?"

I don't know why, but I hadn't thought about this language thing at all. The whole situation seems even more impossible now. "How will she understand us? How will she go to school?"

"No need to be quite so dramatic, sweetie. She'll learn. Your school has a class for English language learners. In a few months, she'll speak pretty well. In a year, she might not even need the special class. Kids your age learn languages fast. You'll catch on to some Spanish, too, I'm sure. I'm the one who's in trouble. My español has gotten rusty."

I see *no* way in which Mom's situation is harder than mine when it comes to this issue. Her DNA may be northern European, but her soul speaks Spanish. She spent a semester abroad in *Spain* when she was in college. Plus, she and Dad always say Spanish is their love language— without it, they never would have met. I, on the other hand, know a couple of curse words and a few songs from a grand total of two trips to Guatemala.

"Luz, I need to ask you a favor."

A favor? This can't be good. I can't help rolling my eyes. "I'll try to be polite to her, if that's what you're worried about."

Mom laughs. "I'm not worried about that at all! You'll be a wonderful sister. After the initial shock and all."

If she'd overheard my thoughts all day, she wouldn't say that.

"Your dad and I talked it over, and I know it'll be a little crowded, but we want you to share your room."

Frown. Frown-er. Frown-est. I thought my mood could not sink any lower, but it does.

Mom goes on. "I know it's not huge, but it's bigger than the other bedroom. And your dad needs that room for his office. His business takes up some space—you know the big printer is in there for landscape plans."

"Then he should rent an office!" I'm raising my voice again, but come *on*. I have to share my home, my parents, and now my room? It's too much.

"Luz, watch your tone. I know this is asking a lot, but we're all in this together, let's not forget. Your dad can't just rent an office. We don't have that kind of money, especially with . . ."

"Another person. Right." I drill my eyes into hers until she looks down.

Mom gulps down her tea, and I sit back.

"I can see you're angry, lovey, and that's normal. But having a sister can be good. It *will* be good. You have to give her a chance. Remember that you're the one gaining something. She's lost everything."

Mom takes her empty glass to the kitchen, and I have to admit that, on the surface, she's right. *My* mom hasn't died. *I* don't have to move. But it's not true that I'm not losing something.

Closet space, for one thing.

I immediately feel terrible for thinking that.

So okay. Maybe it won't be horrific, sharing a room. If I want to be alone, I can go outside. Or to Mr. Mac's. They can't make me share Mr. Mac.

"I just . . . I wish you guys had asked me."

"I just did, Luz."

"No, I mean about bringing her here."

"Honestly, the paperwork has taken so long that I wasn't sure it would happen." She closes the refrigerator and leans on the counter. "Maybe I've been in denial myself."

Hearing her drop the chipper tone actually helps me unbristle. At least we have a week before she comes. And Solana or no Solana, I've got to learn as much from Mr. Mac as possible. I look at the clock. "Can I go across to Mr. Mac's?"

"Okay, but I'm starting dinner. After we eat, let's make some room in your closet. I'll help. Maybe we'll empty out a drawer or two?"

I know I have no choice, so I don't answer.

Warm air blows across my face as I sidestep down our driveway. Spring is sneaking up on us. It's still a lot colder than Guatemala, though. Does Solana even own a coat?

"Luz! Great to see you." Mr. Mac pushes on his cane and stands up from his flat screen. "You and your dad left in a hurry yesterday."

I tell him the news.

He whistles low, then squints as he looks toward the ceiling. "Solana, you say? Interesting."

"What's interesting?"

"Doesn't your name mean 'light'?"

"Luz, yeah."

"And you know what 'sol' means."

"Sun?"

"Quite so. Light and sun. Luz and Solana. You'll be the lights across the street. Y'all may have more in common than you think."

I doubt this will make sharing my room any easier, but I don't say so. I hitch up onto a stool at the workbench.

Mr. Mac clears a couple of tools off the bench and hangs a T-square on its hook. "A sister, mmm. You want my advice, Luz? Be curious. That's how I got into all this." He gestures around the room. "I asked myself, what can I do with a nail? What can I do with a wire? What can I do with a line of code? Even Albert Einstein said that *curiosity* made him great, not talent."

"Didn't he invent the nuclear bomb? He had to have talent."

"Some talent, sure. Though in point of fact, he did not work on the nuclear bomb."

"Oh."

"He did show how mass relates to energy. That's him on the end." Mr. Mac points to a familiar wild-haired man in his lineup of posters. "You may have heard of his equation, $E=mc^2$. It explains not only why a nuclear bomb is possible, but how stars generate light. Before Einstein, we didn't understand the source of sunlight."

It seems odd that something as basic as sunlight was ever *not* understood.

"Which brings me back to your sister, *Sol*-ana." He winks. "My point is, Einstein was deliberately curious. And it helped."

Curious. Okay. I'll try to be curious about Solana. *Will she be nice? What will she think of me? Will we be able to communicate somehow? Does she take long showers and leave no hot water?* "I guess I do have a lot of questions. I mean, I have no idea what it's like to have a sister."

"Your life is about to get interesting, for sure."

"That's the thing, though. My life is *already* interesting. I'm learning here with you, and I'm starting that class . . ." Everything was just starting to be great, and now this. "I kind of wish we could turn off the 'interesting' faucet."

"Haha! You have a neat way of putting things, Luz." He watches me for a second. "Are you ready to try your first program?"

I sit up straighter. "Yes!" It's a relief to think of something else.

Mr. Mac motions me over to a boxlike monitor sitting on top of a fat wedge with a keyboard in it. "Have a seat. This is the first computer I ever worked on. A present for my twelfth birthday. What a beauty."

Mr. Mac's eyes seem to be misting over as he takes a stool behind me.

"The Apple II Plus," he says. "One of the first personal computers to show up under a Christmas tree."

"I thought you got it for your birthday."

"I did, but that Christmas, I wanted it more than anything. My parents could only afford the disk drive in December. I had to wait until my January birthday for the whole computer. Back then, you could get a car for what this baby cost."

"What's a disk drive?"

"This." He pats a box next to the computer. "This is its memory." He flips up a little door on the front and pulls out a flat, black square with a hole in the middle. It's about the size of a greeting card.

"But it's not disc-shaped," I point out. "It's square."

"The outside is square, but inside is a plastic circle. Remember the magnetic tape I showed you? The circle inside here is similar. It's plastic, with magnetic material on both sides. Instead of threading the tape through heads, like the cassette, the disk drive's heads move directly to the right track as this spins. We call it direct-access storage. Do you use a flash drive on your computer?"

I nod. "I have one for school."

"That's a direct-access storage device, too. The computer goes right to the file it needs, without scrolling through whatever's in front of it."

I think I'm following most of this, but I'm glad there's no test coming. I swivel back and forth in the padded chair.

"This disk will save your first program."

"What'll my first program be?"

"You'll write the same first program I did. It's only one line long, but it's the first program all coders write. You'll be part of a grand tradition. Yes, indeed."

15

First, we have to turn it on. Mr. Mac grins as I hunt for the power button. "Here it is!" I flip a rocking switch on the back. A beep sounds, and green letters spell APPLE][on the screen.

"I love this old girl." Mr. Mac looks as if he's tasting his mom's pecan pie.

"Okay so, what will this first program do?"

"It's quite simple. It prints 'Hello World' on the screen. That's it."

"Okay." It sounds easy enough. "But uh, Mr. Mac? The screen isn't working. There's no icons and no mouse pointer. It's just black except those words and that flashing block."

He chuckles. "It's working. We type commands on the screen, and then we run the program and see the result."

"But where's the mouse?"

"No mice here! You'll do everything through typing."

"Is this how programs are written today?" I'm a little worried, wondering if writing old-fashioned code will actually help me in Robotics.

"A lot of today's coding is built on top of code like this. You're getting a look 'under the hood.' If you learn basic commands on this machine, you'll know the patterns that underlie all coding."

I hope he's right. "What do I type first?" I'm ready to fill up that blank screen with *something*.

"First you need a line number."

The thick key makes a *thunk* sound as I type "1."

"Good guess! But in code, as in life, we want to anticipate the unexpected. What if we want to make some new lines of code before your line one?"

"Couldn't we copy-paste it?"

"We don't have that function here. Here you have to leave room between your lines, just in case you decide to add something later. I always make my first line ten."

I see the logic of that. "That leaves room for nine lines?"

"Right."

I type zero, *thunk*, changing my 1 into a 10.

"Now you need a command: PRINT."

With a little help, I get my first program typed in.

```
10 PRINT "HELLO WORLD"
```

"Let's add one more command that clears the screen," Mr. Mac says.

When I type "RUN," the screen clears. Then `HELLO WORLD`, in brilliant green type, glows at the top. A zing shoots to the top of my head. The computer seems alive now, like I've woken it up, and it's greeting the world. Like it's been waiting to meet me.

"Let's do another one!"

Over the next hour, Mr. Mac shows me four more commands. For each one, we practice a tiny program that uses one command at a time.

I quickly learn that the computer takes everything literally. It can't deal with typos. It can't deal with commands out of order. It needs everything neatly laid out, like the notes on Mom's music scores or the stepping stones Dad puts in his landscapes. One note out of place, and I get an error.

I put two commands together, then three. A good program reminds me of the best soccer plays. If every player passes perfectly, dribbles perfectly, the ball lands in the net. But the computer is more predictable than soccer. It never fails to do its job. Only I, the coder, can fail. But I can also fix it.

Finally I type in a program that uses PRINT and all the new commands: LET, DO, WHILE, END.

I check it for typos. I hold my breath and type slowly. "R-U-N." *Thunk, thunk, thunk.* Time to see if I understand all of this. "ENTER."

The screen immediately displays my name in a continuous scroll, cascading down the page. "Yes!" I thrust both fists into the air. I could jump over a house.

Mr. Mac steps back and smiles. "Well done."

Suddenly I understand why Mr. Mac has filled his garage with computers, filled his life with coding. It's fun.

"This is as good as scoring a goal, Mr. Mac."

"Better than a pound cake supper." His eyes smile into mine.

He shifts off the stools and relaxes into his swiveling office chair. "You know, now you can see—computers have a flaw. They don't make room for something new very easily. They can't handle surprises."

I let this sink in. He's talking about Solana. Or maybe he's talking about soccer? "I thought I would play soccer forever." My hand moves to my knee unconsciously. "Dad said I was an athlete. Now I don't know *who* I am."

Along the dark driveway, a line of solar-powered lights starts to glow.

Mr. Mac rubs his chin. "Remember how I said 'the self is not discovered, but created'?" He points at the screen with his cane. "You can build a program; you can build a self. You've already started. On both." He twinkles at me.

I guess? Soccer feels so completely gone now. It's weird. And Solana coming is . . . well, I've never been a sister before. "It's not that easy to build a self," I say.

"No, it's not easy. But into your days, into your life, put things you like. People. Programming. Visits to old Mr. Mac!"

I look down. "Sometimes people just show up."

"I know, Luz. But that's a challenge you can meet. I know you can."

A big "maybe" sits on my tongue, but I don't let it out.

I look for a way to shut down the computer. No mouse, no trackpad . . . "Do I type 'shut down'?"

"Type 'SAVE' first. Your program doesn't save automatically," Mr. Mac says as I type the command. "The disk drive is empty until you deliberately add something." He pulls out the disk, waves it, and winks. "Not discovered, but created."

I get the feeling he's proud of that phrase. "Did you make that up?"

"I did," he says. "See you tomorrow?"

"I hope so," I say. "We have to get ready for Solana."

"That'll give me time to plan your next lesson. Hey, would you like this?" Mr. Mac reaches up to a shelf and unrolls a poster. Six faces float in a light-brown cloud. "I've run out of wall space."

"Who are they?"

"The ENIAC Six. Look them up."

I take the poster, give Mr. Mac a high five.

As I walk across the street, it hits me that I've really started to code. I'm on my way to the Showcase, the robots, and Ms. Freeman's best class. I can't skip or run, but I feel lighter as I climb my driveway home.

16

That night, I type "ENIAC Six" into Google. It turns out they're the women who programmed the first electronic computer, called the ENIAC, during World War II. Electronic Numerical Integrator and Computer. I had no idea that computers even existed that long ago. And in a way, they didn't. If I'm reading this right, the "computer" was actually a bank of switches that had to be individually set by hand. These six math whizzes figured out how to run the system on their own with no computer language, because none had been invented yet.

I click over to a video. A gravelly voice explains that all they had were charts that showed the logic that made switches turn on and off. They were basically thrown into a room with this big bank of switches and told, "Make it do something." I imagine a wall of switches like the one I made with Mr. Mac. What could a computer like that possibly do? I don't find my answer until the last minute of the video. It turns out they programmed it to predict the path of objects, like falling bombs and neutrons traveling through different materials. I'm sad that war had to exist for the ENIAC to exist, but it's cool that these women made it do calculations in thirty seconds that took humans twenty hours.

I find four pushpins to hang the poster right away, but then I remember. Mom said to let Solana help decide wall decorations. Darn it. I doubt she'll want this one up. Unless she's super into math or computers, she won't care a bit about the ENIAC Six.

> > >

Over the next few days, I'm only able to wave at Mr. Mac. Prepping for Solana sucks up a lot of time. Friday afternoon, we move a bunk bed into my room. The next day, Dad adds a fourth hook to the line of coat hooks in the entryway. It takes the whole weekend for us to cram my clothes into half of my closet and two of my drawers.

In the process, we give away a stack of shirts that will be too small for me this summer. "You've grown two inches," Mom says, shaking her head. "Well, it'll be fun to go shopping, then."

"At Target?"

"We'll start at Goodwill, okay? But then Target."

That's about as good as I could hope for.

The days trudge by, each a little harder than the last. A countdown to the end of life as I've known it.

At least there's Intro to Robotics. Crossing the street to the elementary school makes me feel important, somehow. No other kids are trusted to leave the building in the middle of the day. And being with the younger kids isn't as terrible as I thought. (I *am* the tallest, though, and their chairs seem small.) The teacher welcomes me with a pile of parts the first day, and it's fun to follow a diagram to assemble them. But the next day, we do desk work, learning about Newton's laws of motion. Mr. Mac's lessons don't overlap with this stuff. Yet.

"Today's the day," Mom says on Wednesday morning. Like I don't know!

At noon, Solana's plane will land, so she'll be home when I get back from school.

Dad, fidgety all week, paces the floor without eating breakfast. He's giving himself the day off from Véliz Verde to pick her up at the airport.

"I'll come home early, honey," Mom says. "My principal says I can walk out with the students at three-thirty. Are you ready, Luz?" Mom holds my gaze.

I'm like one of those yin-yang circles. White chasing black chasing white, a wheel of excitement and worry. I try to remember what Mr. Mac said. *Be curious.* I let out a deep breath. "I guess?"

"Look, y'all," Mom says. "We have a lot of love in this house. With Solana here, we'll add even more." Her voice shakes like she's not exactly sure this is true, but she wants to be brave. She gathers me into a hug.

Dad comes over, kisses the top of my head, and puts his arms around Mom and me. We stand like a three-legged stool. I wonder if it's the last time.

"You be careful on your knee today," Dad says to me.

Surprise makes me step away. "My knee's been fine for weeks. It only gave way that once the other day."

His brows knit together as if one fall is the same as going back to my cane days. "Don't take risks is what I mean."

"Okay, Emilio." Mom winks at me. "She won't jump off any rooftops today. Got that, Loosey Goosey?"

"I'm not joking," Dad says, his annoyance cutting through the air. "We're lucky she can walk. She has to be careful."

I feel like he's talking about someone else. Someone I was. Someone I'm tired of being. It's like he looks at me and sees nothing but the injury.

"I *am* careful," I say. "Trust me. I don't run. I don't twist. I don't even stop fast. I'm the one who knows how my leg works now. Just let me handle it."

Dad's eyes widen. I can't tell if he's surprised that I pushed back or because his concern is so unappreciated. Mom has told me before that this is how he shows love.

Well, guess what? None of his fretting and worrying feels like love.

"Okay, okay. You handle it, then," he says, like we've agreed on something, even though everything feels wrong now. He looks from Mom to me, like someone else needs to talk next.

Mom squeezes Dad's hand, then ducks out to the car. I put on my backpack.

"Hey, Luz?" Dad says quietly.

I look up.

"I guess I'm nervous today."

Is that an apology? I look into his eyes, and he doesn't look away. "Yeah, I know. Me too."

At school, it's hard to concentrate. I twirl my pencil and bounce my heel on the floor. My mind keeps stepping up to the idea of Solana, then stepping away. Is she on the plane yet? Is she landing? Did she bring everything she owns?

She and Dad did a video call last night, and I could have met her then, but when I heard who it was, I ran outside. I'm not sure why. I just know that my stomach started bubbling, *glub glub glub*. It hasn't stopped.

The final bell rings, and my stomach glubbing speeds up. Somehow, I'm stepping off the bus and approaching the house.

The driveway has never looked steeper.

I open the door to the smell of onion, garlic, and tomato. A welcome dinner, I guess.

"Luz! Come on in here." Dad's mood is the opposite of this morning. If he's nervous, it doesn't show. He seems relieved. Happy, even.

He whisks me to the living room to face a sturdy girl with tan skin who stands a little taller than me. Our eyes meet, and my breath stops. She's actually here. In our house. To stay.

"This is Solana, Luz," Dad says warmly. "Solana, tu hermana, Luz."

Before I can think what to do, Solana pulls me into a hug and kisses each cheek.

Stunned by the kiss thing, I stammer, "Uh, hi." And then, "Hola," which is "hello" in Spanish. That's one word I know.

I take in her knee-length dress, ribbon belt, and white headband. Did she dress up for the trip or does she look like this every day?

"¡Hermana!" Did she say "sister"? Her smile gleams, and her eyes are exactly the shade of Dad's. It's a little weird seeing his brown eyes in her face.

I manage a weak smile. The truth is, I'd imagined ignoring her or living, like, *around* her somehow. Staying out of her way or something. Now I understand how stupid that was. She's so real, 3-D, hi-res, and tall. She'll be part of every meal, every trip, every movie-watching session. She'll be in my room. It's hard to pretend I'm happy.

She lifts her thick hair off her neck and lets it fall behind her shoulders. It isn't just long; it's wide. I tuck my own short, thin hair behind my ears. I never thought much about my hair. A short bob worked great for soccer. But even if I grew it long, my hair wouldn't look like Solana's. There's just not enough of it. She'll probably use up all the shampoo.

We stare at each other, and silence expands between us like an inflatable elephant.

Even if she spoke English, I'm not sure what I'd say. A dark corner of my heart wants to say, *Can't you go back?*

"Why don't you show Solana y'all's room?" From the couch, Mom flashes a shiny smile, like we're all on a Netflix show.

Solana looks at Mom, blinking.

"Tu cuarto," Mom says, pointing down the hall.

Solana doesn't move, but looks at me with raised eyebrows.

Fine. Anything is better than standing here with the inflated Elephant of Silence breathing between us. I motion for Solana to follow.

Though I know she doesn't understand, I start talking. "That's the bathroom," I say as we pass the door, "and this room is ours. It's bigger than Dad's office, at least. You'll see that later." Talking to her feels a little like throwing paper napkins instead of paper airplanes, but maybe hearing English is good.

Inside, I open *our* closet and pull out *her* two empty drawers. "I cleaned these out for you." Oops, I let my tone go grumpy. She can't understand me anyway, right?

But her face tilts to the side in concern. I glue on a smile and over-brighten my tone.

"Which bunk do you want?" I point to the beds.

She bows and opens one arm to me. I think she's letting me choose.

"I'll take the top," I say, taking a few steps up the ladder and patting the mattress. For the last few days, I've been trying out both bunks. I like looking up at the ceiling more than the underside of another bed.

If she's upset at moving or being here or sharing a room, she doesn't show it. Is she really this, I don't know, agreeable? I bet these first-day manners will wear off soon. Then we'll see what she's really like.

Mom and Dad show up in the doorway with her luggage.

"Might as well unpack," Mom says in English. "I mean, oh what's the word? Maleta? Suitcase?"

Dad quickly translates into Spanish. He says something new, too, I guess, because Solana giggles, and he grins back.

"What?" I ask.

"I told her that you made room for her things," he says.

"But what was funny?"

Dad looks like he's going to explain, but then exhales. "It doesn't translate. See, in Spanish, the word for . . . Oh, never mind."

Great. Dad and Solana have a secret already.

"Let's finish cooking dinner," Mom says to Dad. "The girls can get to know each other."

Seriously? How exactly can we "get to know each other"?

Mom sticks her head back in. "We're having arroz con pollo." Her *R*s rumble like a little motor.

Maybe we'll have more Guatemalan food now? That's the first good news in all this. I do like that rice and chicken dish.

Solana unzips her bulging suitcase, and Zigzag inspects everything, nosing the compartments and zippers. "Mish!" she says to the cat, scooping her up in a hug. I know that "cat" is "gato" in Spanish. Not meesh. Maybe this is some sort of nickname for cats in Guatemala? I have to admit, it's sweet.

Solana pulls out skirts and button-downs first—does she go anywhere besides church and maybe, like, orchestra concerts?—but I finally see some jeans. I point to them and give her a thumbs-up.

She nods her permission, and I tuck the jeans into a drawer while she hangs up all the skirts. I remember what used to be in that drawer—*my* jeans—but oh, well.

"Pelota de fútbol," she says, her voice muffled at the back of the closet.

Great. She's found my soccer ball.

With a flick of her foot, the ball rolls out, and with it, the memory of the grass, the run, the crack of my kneecap. I grab it up and march past her to the closet. She asks me something, I can tell by the pitch of her voice. I don't want to talk about why I can't play. I don't want to talk about how I used to play. I definitely don't want to talk about whether she plays. I put the ball on a high shelf this time and ram a stack of board games against it.

I turn around to see Solana's brows draw together. Obviously confused.

"I don't play anymore!" I say too loudly.

She steps back, her eyes wide.

"Yeah, well."

She stands very still.

I close my eyes and let out a deep breath. *Okay, Luz, let's not yell at her on her first day.* "It's not your fault," I say. The Spanish apology pops into my head. "Lo siento." I touch her shoulder so she knows I mean it.

She still doesn't move, and I realize that my one sentence isn't enough. "Here," I say, scootching my pant leg up. The surgery scars speak for me. "Fútbol," I say.

She makes a little gasping sound and nods.

So now she knows. Partly. I'll never have enough Spanish to explain it all. Like, what's the word for "ligament" or "crutches"? Never mind.

"Let's finish this up," I say, kneeling by her suitcase. Maybe I can still get over to Mr. Mac's today. I know she just got here, but I could use a break already.

She unpacks some tennis shoes. Next comes a sketchbook, thick with wrinkled pages and colorful bookmarks hanging out. I try to get a better look, but she holds it to her chest and then stuffs it under her pillow. I don't ask.

Out of an inner pocket, Solana pulls a framed picture. She stares at the woman's face for a long time, then takes a shaky breath. It must be her mother. *Please don't cry. I won't know what to say.*

She looks around for a place to put it.

"Here," I say, hurriedly, pointing to the bedside table. I scoot the alarm clock over and move a couple of seashells from Galveston to my bookshelf.

Her shoulders relax as she positions the frame, and her fingers linger on the edges. Solana's mom has her same big hair.

It's terrible of me, but I can't help wishing this woman were still alive—not for Solana, but for me. Then none of this would be happening.

18

Usually cake is a good thing. But a cake that says ¡Bienvenida Solana! in swooping letters—well, it's not going to be as sweet as usual. The cake sits in the middle of the table all through dinner, while Mom and Dad act like the people who seat you at a restaurant. Polite, polite, polite. I can't relax.

Solana's remarkably calm for being in a new country. She smiles at Mom, she talks with Dad, their Spanish phrases flying back and forth like a Frisbee. They sound comfortable already, probably because of all those video calls that happened I-don't-know-when.

I think of my conversation with Dad this morning, his be-safe sentences landing like bowling balls, my pushback sailing like a cast-iron skillet.

Once we wash the dishes, Dad and Solana start a video call with her aunt in Guatemala. With relief, I pull on my jacket and slip across the street.

"It's Luz!" Mr. Mac waves.

I've never been happier to see old computers and a peg-board of tools. Though I'd never tell Mom and Dad, this garage is more home than home right now.

"Hey, Mr. Mac." I jump up on a stool at the workbench.

"I'm afraid I was just about to close up for the night."

"Oh, darn." My chest sinks in.

"Solana arrived today?" Mr. Mac stands a length of wood against the wall.

"Mmm-hmm." I set my chin on my stacked fists.

"You'll have to bring her over."

No! The word bolts through my brain before I can think. "Uh, I don't think she likes computers and stuff. She wears skirts."

Mr. Mac laughs. "Didn't you look up the ENIAC Six? They wore skirts."

"Yeah, I know." I try to think of some other reason to keep Solana away. It's not nice, I guess, but there's a heat behind my eyes when I think of her here. "She's gonna be really busy. Learning English and all."

Mr. Mac tilts his head but doesn't say anything.

A can of wood stain is the last thing to put away. I reach for it, knowing that it goes in a bin below the workbench. Mr. Mac reaches for it, too, and I see something strange. His thumb. It's thumping, like it's repeating a note on a piano. In fact, his whole hand is waffling back and forth until he clasps the can.

"Are you all right, Mr. Mac? Your hand is moving."

"Oh, that. Nothing to worry about. I'm fine as frog fur." He winks. "I'm just old, Luz."

I wonder. My math teacher is old, and she doesn't shake like that. I hope Mr. Mac is okay.

"You want to hang around while I shut down the computers?"

"I'll help," I say.

Too soon, I'm home again. I duck in and out of the bathroom, brushing my teeth fast, and climb into bed early.

When Solana comes in, I turn to tell her good night. It's her first night, after all, and even though this whole room-sharing is weird, I know it's got to be just as weird for her. Weirder.

She's in a new flannel nightgown. Did her aunt buy it for her? Again, it seems formal and looks stiff; I want to tell her that a T-shirt and leggings is fine for sleeping.

"Buenas noches," she says, meaning "good night." She stands awkwardly for a moment, then climbs under the covers.

"Buenas noches," I say, not sure what else to add. If this were a sleepover, it would be the lousiest one ever.

The next few days are the Twilight Zone. I teach Solana how to layer shirts to keep warmer and how to run the dryer, since she's used to a clothesline. My parents both take a day off from work, a completely unheard-of thing in my life up to now. They register Solana for school, get a tour of the building, and, guess what—go shopping.

And not at Goodwill or even Target. *The mall.* Again, unheard of! I shouldn't be jealous. I have a room full of clothes, and she has a suitcase. But seeing those paper bags with arched handles made me swallow hard. Even though Mom chirped, "We found lots of good sales," there's probably no money left to buy me a pair of socks.

Finally, it's Monday. A normal day. I can't wait for Intro to Robotics class. That's where I feel comfortable. That's where there's no Solana.

"Ready, girls?" Dad asks. "¿Listas?"

Dad's driving us to school, in case taking the bus is "too much" for Solana on her first day. *I* took the bus *my* first day of middle school, and she's two years older than I am, plus I'd be with her. But whatever.

I get out my list as we drive. It's a Tips for Solana list. I want to help her out, because let's face it, even I know first days can be tough. And besides, even though I feel bad thinking it, honestly, truthfully, in my I-know-it's-selfish heart, I'd like it if she didn't embarrass me. I used Google Translate, which isn't perfect, but I hope she'll appreciate it.

"Here," I say, handing it over. She starts reading. This is what I typed in.

TIPS

- **Don't kiss anyone at school. Hugs are okay with a *friend*.**

- **When teachers ask you to introduce yourself, don't feel bad if people laugh. Some people are mean. Just ignore them.**
- **Wait for me at lunch. Don't sit just anywhere in the cafeteria. Certain places belong to certain groups.**
- **Don't pick up anyone's trash for them.**

(At home, Solana springs up and clears the table after every meal. The first time, it was sweet, but now it makes me look like a slacker. Mom even said, "Luz, you could take a page from your sister." Thanks a lot.)

- **The drinks will have ice. This is the USA.**
- **The iced tea will be sweet. This is Texas.**

After a minute, she says, "Gracias, hermana," but her voice sounds more like a wheeze. Maybe she sees it as bossy? Maybe I made her more nervous? I just think if she sits in the jock spot at lunch, she'll be in a mess of trouble. I'm only trying to help.

We drive up to a long, low, brick building, where at least a hundred kids are clustered around the front doors. I glance to see if Solana is freaking out. She's only been here once, to register and meet the ELL teacher. I know I'd be scared.

She's wearing a skirt, but at least Mom got her a sweater that's on-trend—brand-new from Macy's, no less. That should help. Fitting in will be hard enough as it is.

We get inside, and Solana's doing fine. Better than fine. Her head is up, and her shoulders aren't rolling forward. In fact, she's waving to someone.

A girl runs up the hallway and speaks Spanish excitedly. I guess they met when Solana got the tour? Are they friends already?

As they talk, I recognize the Spanish-speaking girl. Her name is Alicia, and she refused to be partners with me last fall in homeroom. At least that's what it seemed like. The teacher put us in pairs, but she switched with someone as soon as she saw me. She better be nice to Solana.

"You good?" I ask my sister. If she is, I'll risk leaving them together.

She gives me a thumbs-up.

I trot across the street, a spring in my step, and the desk lady buzzes me into the elementary building. Mr. Sung dumps gears of different sizes and colors onto our desks. Red, blue, yellow, purple. *Yes!* My hands get happy as I line them up, biggest to smallest. *Maybe my Showcase project should use gears. . . .*

"Grab any two and fit their teeth together." He lets us play with them for a minute. "Now here's our question." Mr. Sung's voice takes the tone of a detective solving a mystery. "If the little one turns ten times, how many times does the big one turn?"

He writes "Calculating Gear Ratios" on the board.

Before the bell rings, I've counted all the teeth on each gear and used division to answer the question. I've also learned that the little gear is the "driver." The big gear is the "driven." Everything clicks together—the teeth and the numbers and the feeling that I already knew this somehow, and Mr. Sung is just reminding me. I hope Solana's day is going this well.

At lunch, the globs of kids look nothing like well-coordinated gears. The cafeteria is a room-size lava lamp, with kid-clumps floating between the tables. Your basic chaos.

I get my tray, then look around for Solana. I promised I would sit with her. She better not be sitting by the Populars' window. Or by the stage where the cowboy-hatted Ropers sit. The borders are ragged, but each group has a kind of headquarters.

I used to sit with the soccer girls, including Skyler, but instead of sitting in the middle like I used to, I've been on the edges for weeks. They don't explain the details of games I miss anymore. And I haven't told them about my computer project. They wouldn't be into it. Anyway, Solana shouldn't have to sit alone. *Where is she?*

Laughter ripples out across the cafeteria from one of the bigger kid-clumps. A crowd huddles around something, and more are gathering. "One, two, three, four!" they shout in unison. What are they counting?

I walk over, still carrying my tray. I almost drop it when I see a familiar face at the center of the circle.

It's Solana. Solana surrounded by about fifteen kids. Solana flicking something into the air.

As I look between shoulders and around heads, I see it's a toy.

She holds a stick attached to a long string with a wooden cup at the end. When she flicks her wrist, the cup jerks into the air and lands on the stick. She does this several times in a row, and the kids count aloud.

Then she gets fancy. With the wooden cup still on the stick, she jerks her wrist. The cup makes a tight rotation and lands back where it was. This, too, the kids count. After ten, everyone cheers, and she hands the toy to another kid. Everyone wants a turn. Even me.

I step back. She doesn't need my help, obviously— there's no way she'll be sitting alone now. Who knew that bringing a kiddie toy to middle school would be such a hit? Maybe I should go find Skyler and the team?

A pair of eyes catches mine from the outer ring of kids. It's the red-shirt boy from Robotics, though today his shirt is green, with a Rubik's Cube on it. His smile is electric. "Did you see that?" he asks.

A tickle races around my stomach as I realize he's talking to me. I nod, setting my tray down.

"She's good." He looks at Solana through the crowd. "Who is she?"

"She's my sister. Half-sister. She just moved here." I can't believe that my first words to this electric-smile boy are about Solana. I change the subject. "You're in Robotics."

"Yeah. Robotics is pretty much why I come to school. Will you be at the club Friday? I've seen you around Ms. Freeman's room."

So he noticed me. "Yeah, I just started the intro class. But I'm hoping to skip to Robotics Two next fall. I loved that Ping-Pong ball thing y'all were doing." I don't mention Mr. Mac and his tech garage. "What happens at the club?"

"We mess around with the computers and robots, and Ms. Freeman shows us extra stuff." He grins.

"Sounds cool." I mean it. I'd love to hang out in Ms. Freeman's room and experiment, especially if I can learn extra stuff. I'll need it for my Showcase project. Maybe I can even see what other kids are planning and get ideas.

"Luz!" Solana's voice rings out. She dashes over, pulls me into the middle of her circle, and presses the toy into my hand. "Capirucho," she says.

I *have* been wanting to try it. How did she know? She's so nice, it's hard to stay annoyed with her.

I take the stick and jerk my wrist, but the wooden cup doesn't land on the stick. It hits my hand, it swings into the air, it thunks my forehead when I bend forward to concentrate. I'm used to being pretty coordinated, but this thing takes practice. I hand it back.

"Can I try?" says Robotics boy.

Solana drops it in his palm. He lets the wooden cup hang at the bottom of the string and waits for it to stop swinging. When it's very still, he flips it up fast. It misses the stick completely, and he laughs at himself as he tries a few more times. Finally, he shakes his head and says, "You make it look easy!"

"Solana," my sister says to him, holding out her hand like a grown-up.

"The name's Trevor," says Robotics boy. Instead of shaking her hand, Trevor offers a fist.

She changes her hand to a high-five, and he meets it with his palm. They're fumbling this hand thing, but they don't seem to care. They both laugh, and she gives him a few pointers on his wrist technique.

How does she do it? She's made her weird into cool. Her New Factor into a Wow Factor. And why can't I talk to strangers the way she does? Is it because she's thirteen? She acts like everyone is already a friend.

I take a deep breath and turn to Trevor. If she can do it, I can.

"I'm Luz," I tell him.

"Lose?" Trevor says, immediately pronouncing my name wrong.

The fact that my name sounds so much like "lose" is the worst. In elementary school, some kids thought it was funny to call me "loser" on the playground. Ha. Ha. And ha.

"It's Luz," I say. "Like loose."

"Got it," he says. Trevor tries the capirucho again, and the wooden cup finally flips onto the stick.

"Yes!" he shouts.

"Nice!" I say.

"Tell your sister she's cool." He tosses the toy, and I catch it.

I'm about to answer with something smart, something clever. *Sure thing, Trusty Trevor. Will do, Trippy Trevor. No problem, Trouncy Trevor. Geez, I'm trying-too-hard, Trevor!* Just "Sure thing" almost reaches my lips when he turns away. His *Star Trek* backpack moves off and disappears through the doorway.

Tell your sister she's cool thrums behind every other thought in my head. How does anyone have a first day like this? Finding a friend at the door, impressing everyone at lunch. In four hours, Solana's already more popular than I am. And without knowing English!

She comes bouncing back to the lunch table, and we eat our chicken fingers. I guess I should be thankful she helped me meet Trevor. I motion to her food with my chin to ask if it's good. "Yes, es bueno," she says, and takes a big bite of potatoes.

Since I can't think of anything to say, I'm relieved when a girl from her ELL class shows up. She and Solana launch into fast Spanish, and I concentrate on my green beans. After a while, I wonder if they even see me anymore. I pull out my math homework and finish it before the bell.

After school, a bright, cloud-free sky greets me out front. Solana sees me, runs over, and opens her arms for a hug.

"Luz!"

I hug her back. "¿Un buen día?" I ask, pulling up "a good day" from some childhood Spanish app. It'll be ninth grade before I have a Spanish class again in school. Why don't they teach languages sooner?

She goes for the kiss thing, but stops herself, thank goodness. She must have had a good rest-of-the-day. Or maybe she's relieved to have it over? Either way, her happy dial is turned up high. I have to admit, between gear ratios and learning Trevor's name today, I'm feeling pretty good myself.

As we wait for Dad to pick us up, I spot a line of kids in front of an open box. Behind it stands a girl with a green sash. Girl Scout cookies! Thin Mints are my favorite. Kids carry away their orange, green, and red boxes as I dig into my pocket. Three quarters. Maybe my coin purse has some bills in it? Yes!

I hold up the money and pull Solana to the line. She understands as soon as she sees cookie pictures on the boxes. She leans into me and does a little hop of excitement. I don't think she's ever heard of acting cool. But I'm excited, too.

"How much?" I ask, when it's our turn.

"Five dollars," the Girl Scout says, neatening her stack of bills.

I count my dollars and quarters. Then Solana's whisper breaks my concentration.

"Three dollars," she says in my ear, pronouncing the O like "dough." *Doh-lars.*

"No, it's five," I whisper back.

She tugs on my jacket sleeve. "Three. Three," she says.

I'm confused. She knows the difference between five and three.

The Girl Scout's face squinches up. "Do you have it?" she asks.

"Yes, Thin Mints, please."

As I hand over three ones and eight quarters, Solana lets loose a patter of whispered Spanish, complete with gestures that I don't understand.

"Wait, Solana."

I'm happy to carry away the green box, but I'm annoyed about Solana. What was all that about?

Dad pulls up in our boxy white car, and we climb in. Solana talks in a sharper voice than I've heard from her before.

Dad laughs and goes into a full minute of Spanish.

When he stops, I say, "Doesn't she understand how to buy stuff? I'm so lost."

"Sorry Luz," Dad says. "She thought you should bargain. It seemed like a situation for debating the price." He chuckles and shakes his head. "Too bad she couldn't save you some money!"

Now I get it. I remember bargaining. In Guatemala, my parents bought papayas at the open-air market and haggled with the vendor over the price. Now I see why Solana was so insistent. She thought we were getting ripped off!

"Pass me up a cookie, would you?" Dad calls from the front seat.

I share two Thin Mints with Dad and offer Solana some. Now her voice is swooping up in pitch, like she can't believe something, and Dad grins. Maybe she's amazed that we don't bargain with Girl Scouts, or maybe she's amazed that she wanted to. When she laughs, I know she understands. I guess it *is* funny.

Spanish fills up the car, and my mind turns to coding. I think of the gears in class and my program on the Apple II+. The thoughts make the cookies yummier.

Finally, Dad finds my eyes in the rearview mirror. "What was *your* day like?" His voice still floats close to laughter. I can tell he's smiling; his eyes crinkle at the edges. It's nice to see him like this. Gone is the worry about my knee. Gone are the questions about whether I did something stupid like cartwheel through the cafeteria. It's just Dad smiling. Smiling at me.

But then it hits me.

She did it. Solana. She's why he's happy. She put him in a good mood; *she's* why at long last it occurred to him to talk to me about something besides my injury. How do I even start? Does he remember that I'm in Robotics now? There's too much to say, and my throat closes. But I have to say *something*.

"Fine." His eyes hold mine for a second, but he doesn't say anything more.

Lucky for me, Mom takes Solana for a haircut
after school. As soon as they leave, I'm out the door to Mr.
Mac's.

Full sun warms my face, and I see that trees up and
down the street are doing their branch magic, pulling
leaves out of their sleeves.

"How was Intro to Robotics today?" Mr. Mac asks right off.

I tell him about gear ratios, and he listens carefully.

"And did Solana have a good first day?" he asks.

I kind of came here to get a break from thinking about
her, but she made this question easy. "Yeah, she really did.
She's some kind of people-genius."

"Good for her! I never liked first days myself."

"Me neither."

"Let me show you what I'm working on. Have you heard
of a chat bot?" Mr. Mac points to a chair in front of a large
monitor with a cursor blinking at the top. I take a seat.

"I built a simple one. Go ahead and talk to it. Well, *type* to it."

I type "Hi," and soon I'm in a conversation with a computer program. It asks all about me and even makes jokes. Sometimes it repeats itself, or says something that doesn't quite make sense, but it's still pretty good.

"How did you make this?" I ask.

"I mostly used commands that you already know. Come see the flowchart."

My chair has wheels, so I roll over to another computer, where Mr. Mac brings up a flowchart with color-coded branches. It has everything the chat bot says and key words the user might respond with.

"These asterisks are for when it doesn't matter what the human types. The chat bot responds with one of these phrases: "That's interesting" or "Tell me more.""

Mr. Mac turns to me. "Would you like to make one of these? My plan is for you to code one more program on this Apple II Plus dinosaur and then start on a new language: Scratch."

"Aww, I like the dinosaur."

"Me too. But it's good to learn a language that people are using in this century." He laughs at his own joke. I love how happy he makes himself. "Today, let's stick with what you know. Your chat bot could be a chef who talks to people about recipes or a toy recommender for parents. If you're willing to type in a lot of toy names, that is."

"Or a fortune-teller!" I say. One of our neighbors dressed up as a fortune-teller last Fourth of July and did palm reading at FourthFest. I think she made up everything she said, but it was fun.

"Why, sure! What would you tell people?"

I try to picture it. "They'd ask for advice, and I'd tell them something wise, like fortune cookies do. Oh, but then I would need a bunch of fortunes, and I'd have to type them all in." I don't want to do all that typing for a one-answer thing. I swivel back and forth in my chair. What would be simpler, but still fortune-teller-y? "I've got it! I'll make a Magic 8-Ball!"

"Bingo!" says Mr. Mac. "That's the black ball toy that answers questions, isn't it?"

"Yup, but you have to ask yes-no questions. Like, 'Will I get a horse for my birthday?'" I had two Magic 8-Balls when I was little because two kids brought them as birthday presents.

"How will you start?" Mr. Mac says. He likes to let me figure things out.

"The computer has to tell the person—"

"The user."

"Yeah, the user. The computer needs to print, "Please ask your yes or no question," on the screen. Or how about 'You may approach! Ask your yes-no question.'"

"I like it." Mr. Mac's eyes twinkle.

"Then, from all the possible answers, it needs to pick one to print on the screen."

"How many answers are there?"

"Mmm. Ten? Maybe twenty?"

"Let's go back a step. How will the computer know that the user has finished asking their question?"

"Oh. I better have the user press ENTER or RETURN. The computer should wait for that signal to spit out the answer."

Mr. Mac's pleased with me. I can tell because he rocks back and forth on his heels, anchored by his cane. It's sort of a whole-body nod. "And how will the program end?"

"The computer could say, 'Have a nice day.' Or, wait, that *Star Trek* phrase: 'Live long and prosper.'"

"Sounds like you have a plan, Luz."

In about ten minutes I have a list of answers the computer will give the user. YES, NO, TOTALLY!, COULD BE, LOOKIN' LIKE NO, LEANIN' TOWARD YES, HARD TO SAY, COME AGAIN?, WHEN PIGS FLY! Some are from the real Magic 8-Ball, but most I make up myself. I start coding, starting with a new command I've learned: CLR. It clears the screen.

I work with the commands I know, and Mr. Mac helps make the answer random with a piece of code he calls a randomizer.

As I type in commands for a loop, I wonder if a virtual Magic 8-Ball will be good enough for a Showcase project. I'd love to have Trevor ask my 8-Ball a question. But then

I imagine showing Ms. Freeman. No, I think I need something more sophisticated.

Mr. Mac's extra lights come on in the garage, and I realize it's getting late. I've just about got it, though. I type another line and finally "220 END" and "SAVE." I'll have to do testing and debugging tomorrow, I guess.

It can't hurt to run the first test now, though. "RUN," I type.

`YOU MAY APPROACH! ASK YOUR YES-NO QUESTION.`

So far, so good. I type my question.

"WILL I THINK OF A GREAT SHOWCASE PROJECT?" ENTER.

`HARD TO SAY. LIVE LONG AND PROSPER.`

It worked!

"Mr. Mac! Look! I did it!" I'm so excited I spin around three times in the chair. Happy, happier, happiest.

"Brilliant! Let me try it." Mr. Mac rolls over from his computer and types in a question.

"IS LUZ LEARNING FASTER THAN A SNEEZE THROUGH A SCREEN DOOR?"

`TOTALLY! LIVE LONG AND PROSPER.`

Mr. Mac gives me a high five, and my chest expands with pride. This is my most complicated program yet, and it ran the first time!

"Maybe you can add Spanish text tomorrow. So your sister can use it."

"Oh." I hadn't thought of that.

He rolls back to his computer. "I'm always thinking of ways to improve my programs."

I can believe that. "But Solana may not ever come over here."

"Well, that would be too bad. I'd never meet her."

How can I say that's my whole plan? I keep my answer vague. "If she comes, I'll add the Spanish."

"Good deal," he says with a clap.

I shut down the computer. I'm still glowing with the pleasure of a good program when I run toward home. Well, not run, but walk fast. And skip a few times on my good leg. I'm surprised I don't fly a bit with every step, I feel so good.

I get another zingy feeling as I imagine showing Mom and Dad. Maybe Mom will take a picture and share it with her friends online. Maybe Dad will brag to his friends that his daughter is becoming a coder. I can't wait to tell them.

I burst into the warm room, ready to tell Mom and Dad that I coded a Magic 8-Ball.

But the house is quiet. No one's at the table or in the living room. Zigzag rubs my shoe with her head and meows. "Hey, girl," I say. "How's my ZZ? Where is everyone, huh?"

Then I hear a sound I haven't heard in months. It's my father's voice ringing out a long, high pitch. "¡Goooooooooaaaaaaal!"

My heart stalls.

I open the back door, and there they are. Mom guarding a space between two watering cans that mark a goal, Dad and Solana playing soccer. Solana dribbles the ball, kicks left-footed to fake Dad out, then takes off at a run—a full, free, top-speed run—toward the two trees that Dad and I always used for a goal. As she speeds past, I remember what running feels like. My legs ache to run, too. Tears threaten to fall, but I blink them back.

Then I see the haircut. That was no trim Solana got. Her hair is a foot shorter, cut just like mine. When she crosses the goal line and turns around, she pants and bends forward to brace her hands on her knees. Her face glows, and her hair flounces around her face in the wind. It's my hairstyle, but more beautiful than cute. She's me, only better—soccer and hairstyle and working knees. Luz 2.0.

Dad calls out to me, breathing hard and wearing a sloppy grin. He doesn't say *Come play*. He doesn't say *You could be goalie*. He says, "Luz, we got smoothies. Yours is in the freezer."

Now the tears do come, and I'm glad to rush inside, pretending that I'm desperate for a smoothie.

The three of them tumble in behind me and say happy things, fun things, wasn't-that-great type of things in Spanish. That's what it sounds like, anyway.

Solana says, "¡Hola, Luz!" and tries to hug me, but I shrug her away. I can't possibly explain, but I can't possibly hug her either. She pulls back and goes to wash her hands.

"I hope you don't mind that we got out your soccer ball," Mom says to me. "Solana asked if your dad played at all, and their chat morphed into a little game."

"We were very careful, though," Dad adds. "I went easy on her." He winks.

None of this makes me feel better. They're missing the point. I want to run too, play too, make them proud, score a goal, feel like the whole yard is lit by happiness. Like it used to be.

Solana comes back and pulls chilaquilas out of the oven.

"Look at this, Luz," Mom says. "Solana made them herself. We picked up the ingredients on the way home. Doesn't it look delicious?"

How does she know how to make complicated food, while I can only do mac and cheese? "Delicious," I say flatly. I usually love chilaquilas, with the cheese all melty inside the fried squash, but the thought of eating anything, especially anything made by Solana, makes me queasy.

"I bet she would teach you to make it," Dad puts in.

What is this, Solana Appreciation Day?

We sit down to eat, and I shove food around on my plate as a half-Spanish, half-English conversation gets started. They have plenty to talk about. Apparently, the haircut was emocionante and the smoothie place was emocionante and soccer was emocionante. Everything to Solana is exciting. I don't even bring up my Magic 8-Ball code. Then they move on to talk of school.

"Wow," says Dad, obviously attempting to draw me into the conversation. "Sounds like Solana really made an impression with the capirucho! What a good idea, bringing that the first day."

"She's amazingly social. I was never that brave," Mom says. "Luz is more like me. A little shy." She translates for Solana.

I look up from my plate. "I'm not shy."

"I just mean when you first meet people, sweetheart."

My eyes cut to Solana. "Well, yeah, I don't bribe them with toys or anything. I give them some space."

"'Bribe'? Aren't you being a little harsh?" Mom asks.

I lower my voice. "It's not like all those people will be her actual friends." I don't want anyone to translate that.

Solana looks at me, reading my tone. She starts in with a new subject, it seems like, and the word "Trevor" sticks out. I listen harder. Her voice makes a dramatic soundtrack— loud, then soft, then climbing up in pitch. She gestures with her hands. She keeps looking at me, like she thinks it's a topic I'll like. My parents respond with oohs and "¿De veras?" which means "Really?"

"So who is this Trevor?" Dad asks me. "Do I need to meet his parents? Is he an upstanding young man?" Dad's tone is mock serious, with teasing underneath, but I can feel my face turning red.

"He's just a kid at school, Dad."

"That's not what Solana says."

I throw a dark look at Solana. What is she trying to do to me? Doesn't she know this is the kind of thing we DON'T tell the parents?

"He only just learned my name today!"

"Calm down," Mom says. "You're too young to worry about boys anyway. Plenty of time for that."

"Give me at least ten years to prepare, Luz," Dad says. "But it's cute, don't you think, Diana?" He and Mom chuckle.

Do they think I'm a baby now? "It's not cute!" I say. "He's just a Robotics kid." Solana seems to realize that she's started something tense because she drops her hands to her lap. And she's right. She never should have mentioned Trevor. She never should have gotten out my soccer ball. She never should have come.

"Anyway," I say, "Trevor said to tell Solana she's *coo-woll*." I stretch the word "cool" and add a sarcastic *W* in the middle. "He doesn't even like me. He likes *you!*" I spit the sentence at Solana, not knowing if she understands, and not caring either. "Does anyone here care that I did something cool today? Apparently not. Everyone likes you, Solana. Everyone but me."

"Luz!" Mom and Dad say together.

I already know. They can't believe I could be so rude. They can't imagine why I might be mad. Solana can't either. I've never felt so alone, so shoved to the side. They're still staring at me, like my nose is upside down.

"I think you better apologize, and then clear the table for us," Mom says. She looks at Dad, who nods. They've tuned in to a psychic How We'll Punish Luz channel. "Let's have a talk after you brush your teeth."

A talk is worse than regular punishment. "Just give me more chores or something."

"Chores won't cut it, Luz. Think how Solana feels right now. She hasn't done anything to you, and you're yelling at her? I expected better from you." Mom holds out her plate for me to take. "Apology first," she says.

"Lo siento," I say, looking past Solana's left shoulder, obeying the letter of Mom's law. I'm pretty sure I don't sound sincere.

I stand up and walk around the table, picking up plates and forks. Solana touches my arm, but I ignore it. Mom and Dad don't notice. I don't want to be mean, but I can't help it. Solana cooks, plays soccer, wins over everyone, makes my parents forget about me. Why am I even here?

I squeeze the toothpaste so hard that it gloops out three inches of white paste. I know I shouldn't be mad, but what can I say? I'm totally fine that this beautiful, social, uninjured girl is here taking my place? I rinse and spit out the water in a hurry. The Parents Await. Let's get this over with.

Mom and Dad never yell. It's one of the weirdest things about my family. Unless he's cheering at a soccer game, Dad's voice stays even. Unless she's thrilled about a new piece of music or her band winning a marching contest, Mom's voice stays calm. But volume doesn't mean every-thing, let me tell you. Nothing can make me feel worse about myself than soft sentences from these two.

I walk into the living room and immediately see Zigzag curled up on Mom's armrest, like she's on their side. *You too, ZZ?*

All their words to me are quiet, controlled. They're very disappointed. Shocked. Et cetera.

When they ask why I'm unhappy, I don't know what to say. Her chilaquilas were too good? I can't point to a single mean thing. She's perfect. It's me who's annoyed, ungrateful, unfair. Finally I tell them, "I wish I could have played soccer with you."

"We could all play a board game on Saturday," Mom offers. *All*. With Solana. Of course. I don't know how to say that this family feels too big now, too full.

"Did you say you did something cool today?" Dad asks.

This is it. This is the moment I wanted to have three hours ago. But nothing feels like it did before. "I just coded something," I say to the floor.

"What was it?" Mom still looks disappointed in me.

Dad looks mostly tired.

This is not how I pictured this announcement at all, but I go ahead and say it. "I made a virtual Magic 8-Ball. You can ask it questions. You know, like a yes-no question."

"That sounds nice," Mom says.

Nice?

I look at Dad. "Don't you have one of those, though?" he says. "An 8-Ball, I mean? I thought you had two."

My chin quivers, and I take a deep breath to make it stop. "Yeah, but . . ." My throat swells with trying not to cry. I can't believe I thought that that simple program would make them proud.

"I'm sure it's really neat, sweetie," Mom says. "And I wish we had heard your news at dinner, but it's still no reason to be rude to Solana."

"No, it isn't," Dad adds.

At last, I'm "excused." I drag my feet down the hall, savoring it as the only stretch of floor with no parents and no Solana. I stop before turning the doorknob to our room. A surge moves through me, and I switch from sad to mad. Since Solana came, I've always been wrong, always not good enough. Well, fine. She has to live here, but I don't have to applaud everything she does. I don't even have to talk to her. Especially not tonight.

I stride in, not even looking at her. I jump into my top bunk and lie down facing the wall.

A minute passes. Another.

I hear Solana turn, the covers rustling.

Does she wonder what she's done wrong?

She can keep wondering.

Tuesday is like an identical twin of Monday, with Trevor practicing Solana's capirucho, talking to her more than me, and the ELL girls hugging on her. I've never had friends like that.

After school, I escape to Mr. Mac's, leaving Solana alone with her homework. I practice the new commands I've learned, but I can't bring myself to start a new project. Mr. Mac notices, but I don't want to explain. What would I say, anyway? My new sister is too nice, too popular, and too good at getting my parents to like her? She *is* like the sun. Bright, extra bright, extra-extra bright. Outshining me.

At dinner, I try to stay perfectly civil, perfectly polite. Solana picks up the dirty plates before I can even think of it, making me look bad again. When she gets to me, I pull the plate away. "I can get it," I say. To make the point, I stand up and gather the water glasses.

"I'm going to take Solana to the library," Dad announces. "She hasn't been there yet, and she'll be able to check out some books in Spanish. Tonight they're open until nine."

"I want to go," I say. I love the library.

"I'm going to take Solana on her own this time, okay Lucita?" Dad says.

"Why?"

"Your dad needs some time with her," Mom says. "You and I can do something here, if you want."

"No, I want to go to the library. I might find some computer books." I can't recall my parents ever discouraging books before.

Solana is standing by the door, reaching for her jacket. I think she's pretending not to hear.

"Luz, try to understand," Dad says quietly. "I haven't been there for her all these years. I'm trying to make it up to her." His eyes are full of concern, but not for me.

"What about me?" I say.

"You and your mom can play a game or something."

Play a game? Why do they keep suggesting this? This isn't about me needing to be entertained. It's about being with my dad. "You never do anything with me anymore. Even before Solana, you worked every Saturday. You can't just give me to Mom. I'm your daughter, too."

"Luz, what are you saying? Of course you are." He looks confused, but I can't see why.

"Then stop ditching me!" I cross my arms.

Dad looks at Mom, who throws up her hands.

Dad sighs. "Well, I'm not sure I should reward this behavior, but I guess you can come. I didn't think it was that big a deal."

Solana can't pretend anymore. She's done fussing with her jacket and its zipper. Her eyes look a little spooked, like maybe she's afraid of me. Somehow I don't want to go now. Obviously, she'll be happier if I don't.

Dad says something in Spanish that I don't understand. Probably he's apologizing that her sister is wrecking yet another evening.

"Never mind," I say, and stalk off to my room. *Our* room. At least I'll have it to myself for an hour or so.

I hear the car start and back out of the driveway. I almost cry, but I pace my room until the feeling passes. With a speed that surprises me, I yank out some note-cards and write all the Apple II+ BASIC commands I know, one per card. On notebook paper, I write out the program that prints my name over and over on the screen. "Luz" may mean light, but tonight I feel like a flame in danger of going out.

The phone rings, and Mom gets into a long talk. Her voice gets loud, and I think I hear my name. I crack open my door to listen.

"Miranda, it's way harder than I thought. She's not a bit of trouble, but it's hard to feel close to someone you don't know. And Luz is impossible. I know it's only been a few days, but . . ."

I close my door. I don't want to know what else she'll say. It's kind of nice to know that Mom is struggling, too, that she's not quite as together as she seems, but I feel bad about being "impossible."

Suddenly, I'm totally tired. Completely drained. I brush Zigzag and put myself to bed early. I turn off the light, crawl under the covers, and hope no one tries to come talk sense into me.

When the door opens slowly, I blink and come to. I must have fallen asleep for real. I hear Solana lie down and adjust her blanket. The whole house goes silent.

Then a muffled *hic* meets my ear. A sniffle. A gulping of air. *Is she . . . ?* Then a single sob and ragged breaths.

She's crying.

25

At first, I'm annoyed, but Solana's tears make my hard thoughts go soggy. My own eyes mist over, partly for her, partly for me. None of this is easy. If I'm totally honest, I'm kind of mad that now I can't stay mad, which hardly makes sense, but it's true. I can't leave her there, though, crying alone. The library thing wasn't her fault anyway. I climb down and kneel next to her.

"Solana," I say.

She buries her face in her pillow.

"Solana," I try again. Can I blame her for not wanting to look at me? I guess I've been pretty rotten.

"Hermana," I say. Sister.

Now she looks up, her face blotchy in the dim glow of the night-light, her dark eyes shiny with tears. When her eyes find mine, I'm met by two pools of sadness. The last of my anger crumbles. "Lo siento," I say. "Lo siento." This time, I mean it.

She hiccups some words, and I realize that we're going

to have to be able to talk. For the first time, I really want to understand her. And for her to understand me.

Google Translate is all I can think of. There's probably an app that would do better, but there's no time to download. I grab my tablet.

Why are you crying? I type.

She lets out an exasperated sigh, but she taps the keyboard. **Why do you hate me?**

I don't hate you, I type. This isn't completely true, and she knows it. I try again. **I don't know. I never had to share my room.** I know it looks silly, and her slow shrug confirms it.

I guess I have to tell the truth. I'll have to tell her more, a lot more, starting with yesterday's backyard soccer game. I type sentences almost faster than Google can translate. **When I saw you playing soccer**, I begin. I tell her about my school team and the Tri-City League, about Dad coaching, about my leg getting messed up, about Dad not talking to me anymore. I even tell her that my soccer friends aren't really friends now.

That sounds very hard. I am sad to hear this, she types.

Thanks.

I remember your scars. That must have hurt!

It feels safe to say something risky. I type fast before I chicken out. **When you and Dad speak Spanish, I feel left out.**

She frowns. **But I am excluded from everything ELSE.**

125

The translation makes her sound formal, but wow, of course. She's right. Everything happens in English. **I wish my Spanish were better.**

Or my English.

You're doing great at school, though, I say.

That was the plan.

"What plan?" I say aloud.

My aunt made me promise something, she types. **She told me that people here can be mean to immigrants. We heard of kids punished for speaking Spanish.**

Oh. **So you decided . . .**

My aunt said to be extra friendly. Convince the kids to like me. And your parents—she said our dad was not very nice.

Dad not nice? I mean, *I'm* not too happy with him right now, but most people would say he's nice. Then I picture Solana's mother, raising her daughter alone. Of course they would think he was a jerk. **Because he left Guatemala.**

Yes. Before he even knew I existed. My mother vowed to never tell him about me. She was angry that he disappeared without telling her he was leaving.

I nod. Solana must have been afraid to come here. She must have worried that we wouldn't accept her, much less love her.

My aunt said to make sure you and your mom liked me. "Show that you were raised well. Clean up after yourself. Help cook," she said. She thought you might be mean.

This aunt is one smart lady. And she was right about me. I'm a terrible sister so far.

But I have failed. Solana sniffs as tears leak out again.

No you haven't. Everyone thinks you're great. Except you.

Our eyes meet. She wants me, Luz, to like her. It seems silly now, but I thought that with everyone else liking her—Dad and Mom and the kids at school and Trevor—she didn't really need *me* to. And somehow, here she is, still wanting to like me—still wanting *me* to like *her*—despite everything. My lip quivers, and I feel my eyes tearing up. **I do think you're great. Maybe too great.**

What am I doing wrong?

I'm sorry. You're not doing anything wrong. It's me. I guess I've been jealous.

She reaches out her hand, and I let her squeeze my shoulder.

When she turns back to the tablet, she types, **I can imagine that. You've always been alone.**

I let this sink in. It's true, of course. I've never had to share my parents or my room. Or anything. Is that why this has been so hard?

It occurs to me that I've never asked her about back home. **Do you miss your mom? Do you miss Guatemala?**

SO MUCH! She layers her hands on her heart.

But you act so happy. So friendly.

She stops to think, brushing her bangs off her face. **I want to cry every day. I have a big loneliness. I miss my favorite foods, my cousins, the bedroom we shared. Too many things to count!** She wipes her nose with her sleeve. **Luz, you don't know me yet, but I am quality,** she says.

I smile at the awkward translation. I think she means "cool." **I know you are.**

You didn't give me a chance.

"Tienes razón," I say, recalling the Spanish for "You're right."

She holds my gaze, and I see a gentleness in her eyes. The air feels cleaner somehow, like the smog between us has cleared. Not everything is fixed, but I feel better than I did.

Your haircut looks good, I type, trying to say something nice and also true.

I wanted it like yours.

"Oh!" This is a surprise. I don't even know what to type.

You're the perfect American girl. You know about Girl Scout cookies! Also, my mom never let me cut my hair short.

I scoot closer to her. **Your mom. You must think about her a lot.**

She tells about the two of them singing Ricardo Arjona songs on walks. She says they loved to try out new recipes together in their little white kitchen with one red wall.

Did you make chilaquilas together?

Solana nods.

Suddenly I want to give her something, something besides a promise to be nicer. I wonder . . . **Do you like computers?** I ask.

"Sí, me gustan," she says, meaning yes.

For real? I mean programming and stuff. Coding. I want to be clear.

I learned some Python from my aunt. She's a web designer.

"What? Seriously?" I say aloud in English. Here she was, knowing some programming, and I was dissing her. *Not your best call, Luz.* I type as quickly as I can. **Friday, after school. There's a club we have to go to. A robotics club. I'll take you.**

She looks up, her eyes curious.

It's going to be amazing.

After school on Friday, I actually can't wait to bring Solana to Robotics Club. It's my first time, too, but I know it'll be great, and somehow sharing it makes it even better. With only ten minutes before it starts, I find Solana outside the library doors.

But she's not alone. She's in a huddle of girls.

None of them steps aside to let me into their circle as I walk up to them. Kind of rude, if you ask me, but never mind. We're on our way to the club!

"Let's go, Solana," I say, tugging her wrist.

"Esta es mi hermana, Luz," Solana says, introducing me as her sister.

One of them looks from me to Solana and back again. "No se parece a ti."

I'm not sure what that means, but it doesn't sound like a compliment. The girl follows up her comment with a shrug, and I'm sure she said something like "She's a pain" or "She's interrupting." But who cares? "Solana, the club," I say.

She holds up a "wait a sec" finger, and the other girls keep right on talking.

"It starts in five minutes," I say, a little louder. "Cinco minutos." I'm so glad Mom drilled the numbers in Spanish with me when I was little.

"Lo siento," Solana says, apologizing. But not to me. To *them*. She says one more thing and they all laugh—at me? I probably do look a little intense. I'm just excited to get To. The. Club!

Finally she pulls away and waves goodbye. As we speed-walk to Ms. Freeman's room, I can't help feeling annoyed with those girls. Talk, talk, talk. They completely ignored me, when it was clear that I was saying something important. Solana's nice to everyone, maybe too nice, but wow, they're obnoxious.

Right at 4:00, we walk past R2-D2—or I do. Solana stops to touch his round head. I think she would hug him and kiss his cheeks, if he had cheeks.

Trevor trots over. "Hey, y'all made it! Come see what I'm building."

He leads us to a tray of LEGO parts, but not the regular-colored bricks I have at home. These are wheels, gears, and sticks, I'd call them, lengths of gray plastic with holes.

"I'm attaching this new sensor to the block." Trevor says, connecting a small white cube to a rectangular block with a black cord. "The hard part is telling the robot what to do with the input."

Half my brain is trying to keep up with him, but the other half is marveling at the thing he's holding.

"So that's the robot?" I ask.

"Yup. Its brain, anyway. Ms. Freeman calls it a microprocessor, but I call it a block. Block*head*, sometimes."

Solana picks up a bare one and turns it over in her hands. It must be on because a green light glows around its buttons. She presses a few and watches the screen change.

"You can add wheels and a motor, plus sensors. But it won't do anything without a program."

"You mean a computer program?"

"Yeah. The instructions. *Detailed* instructions. I use Scratch."

Scratch! That's the language Mr. Mac talked about teaching me.

"I'm so glad you're here, Luz!" Ms. Freeman appears behind us. "And who is this?"

"Solana," I say. "She's my sister from Guatemala."

Ms. Freeman does a little head bow. "Mucho gusto, Solana."

"¡Habla español!" Solana beams, obviously pleased.

"You speak Spanish?" I say.

"A fair amount."

They exchange lots of words, lots of smiles, lots of Lots Of.

"Listen up, everyone." Ms. Freeman claps her hands, and I'm startled to notice that kids are scattered all over the room. I didn't hear them come in. Their heads all turn to Ms. Freeman. "The Showcase is in eight weeks. Let's hear a project update from each of you, and then I'll get out of your way. Oh, and we have two visitors."

Ms. Freeman introduces Solana and me, then the first kid talks about his project for the Showcase. He's making a robotic arm that can draw a hypo-something. I didn't catch the word, but it sounds like a spirograph pattern. Several are making battle bots that will try to ram each other off the blue mat and throw things. Trevor says his project is top-secret, but it will use the motor, the color sensor, and a lot of beams and gears. I have to say, I'm excited by it all, but a little intimidated.

Solana is listening closely, especially when Ms. Freeman translates. Or tries to translate. The words aren't easy to understand even in English. Studded beam, axle joiner, bushings. They're all new to me.

Ms. Freeman dismisses us for free time, and everyone turns back to either their computer or their bot. Instead of jumping up and getting a bot to experiment with, I slump into a chair. It's starting to hit me: eight weeks. Is that all I have? Will I have to know as much as Trevor does? Maybe I was wrong to think I could learn anywhere close to enough. I haven't even started the programming part. The hard part.

Solana touches my shoulder, and I turn to see her look of concern.

"I'm okay," I tell her. "It's just there's this end-of-year..." *Oh yeah. Speak Spanish.*

"Hay un..." I start. Of course the word "showcase" is not on the amazingly short list of Spanish words in my head. Maybe mercado? That's "market." My parents should have taught me Spanish!

"¡Feria!" I say, not sure where I've heard it. I think it means "festival," but close enough.

"¡Una feria! ¡Qué bueno!" she says brightly.

"Y una competición." This word is a guess. Lots of long words like "competition" come out the same in Spanish.

Solana nods, but corrects me, "Una competencia. ¿Y tú?" Solana asks.

She's asking if I'll be in the competition. That's been my goal, but today makes me doubt I can learn fast enough. I look around the room. LEGO trays, a bot following a line of tape, kids coding on computers. I'm useless with a bot right now. I don't know a brick from a beam. But somehow, I'm still happy to be here. It's a weird feeling.

"Yes," I say. "Sí."

Saying it makes me believe it. I *will* be in the Showcase. Even if I'm not a star, or even average.

But I need a program. I say it in Spanish. "Necesito un programa." Again, I'm lucky with the words, remembering "I need a," and stumbling on to a word that's similar in both languages: "program."

"¿De computadora?" She grabs my arm and does a little jump, squealing a phrase I can't grasp at all. Maybe she thinks I already know how to program.

"But I'm new," I say. "New to all of it."

"New?" Solana asks. "¿Nueva?"

"Nueva," I say.

"Yo también soy nueva," she says.

Wow, yes. Not totally new to programming, but new to school, to English, to Texas. And look at how she's jumping right in and trying everything.

So yes. I want to do this Showcase thing. And yes, I want to get into the advanced class. And yes, it's going to be hard, but I have to try. I turn to Solana and Trevor, both handling one of the white plastic blocks.

"Trevor, what's the first thing to know about this bot?"

"Um." His eyes meet mine, and he stalls.

"What?" I ask.

He quickly turns away. "Solana's already on it!" he says. He leans in to help her with some buttons.

She didn't ask for his help, but okay. I lean in, too, trying to learn what she's doing.

"Let's add motors," Trevor says. This time he hands them to me. "Don't they look like little steamrollers?"

"They do!" I say. We add the two motors and learn how to make them spin in different directions.

Next, he reaches over to flip a piece that Solana attached backward. They laugh together.

I'm not surprised that he likes her better. This is the

new story of my life. He can still teach me a lot, though; that's the most important thing. I do catch myself noticing how his loose curls fall just above his kind eyes, and how his laugh makes me want to laugh, too. I get that tickly feeling in my stomach again.

But I focus on two things I didn't know before. One: Mr. Mac is right that I need to learn Scratch. Two: When I go to Mr. Mac's tonight, I'm bringing Solana. If she already knows some Python, she'll love his garage. And she might be able to help me, too.

27

Dad sputters up to the school in his lawn-care pickup truck. It's not that landscaping isn't a cool job or anything, but the truck is as long as three cars and as loud as four. Its trailer bed, loaded with lawn mowers and weed eaters, stretches for miles, it seems like, and the muffler rumbles so loud that we have to shout to be heard even inside the cab. I wish he'd brought the white car, or the Véliz Verde minivan that he uses to check on workers around town. This pickup is from the old days, when his business was small.

We climb in the truck, with me squished in the middle.

"A good day, girls?" Dad shouts. He squeezes my shoulder. When we saw each other this morning, he offered to take me to the library sometime soon. It was nice to hear, though there's definitely still some weirdness between us. At least he's not asking about my leg.

"Yeah, good day," I yell. It's too hard to talk over the engine noise. Even Solana just waves.

I'm glad we can't talk, because after the 8-Ball Announce-ment Fiasco, I'm not ready to tell him about Robotics Club or my Showcase plan. Besides, he might give me that sad face—the one he tries to hide when I do anything besides soccer.

Maybe I can unveil my big coding project when it's done and make him see that I can be good at something else, too. Not just a simple 8-Ball, but something impress-ive. I think that's what he wants most. For me to be really great at something. Something he can be proud of.

At home, Solana and I drop our backpacks inside the door and head for the kitchen. I open the pantry. Not much in there except some round, hard, pancake-looking things that Dad brought from the Central American grocery. I'm not sure what they are. I check out the fridge. We're in luck! There's leftover cake, and a note from Mom saying, "Go ahead and eat the welcome cake. Snack rules waived today. ☺" Her list of approved snacks is flipped over to the blank side.

This time, the cake is a perfect ten on the sweetness scale. We both eat the icing flowers first.

As I eat my last bite, Solana disappears down the hall. She comes back with something in her arms, something I've seen once before. Her sketchbook.

I don't know if it's been under her pillow since that first day, but now she opens it.

Guatemalan scenes fill the pages. Purple volcanoes, a canoe on what has to be Lake Atitlán, and close-ups of a marimba. I'm stunned by the realism. Everything looks three-dimensional.

The most eye-catching page shows huge kites, tall as houses, decorated with all kinds of patterns.

"What are these?" I ask, my voice coming out breathy with awe.

"Barriletes de Sumpango."

"Dad has talked about this!" I remember him saying that he went to Sumpango as a kid to see giant kites. He said they were big, but whoa. I had no idea.

"Para el Día de los Difuntos y Todos los Santos."

"For the day of the . . . what?"

Solana makes an *X* on her chest with her arms and then makes a hilarious face by rolling her eyes back and letting her tongue loll out from one side of her mouth. Hey, she's funny! I feel bad I hadn't noticed that yet.

"Oh, okay. The Day of the Departed, right? And All Saints Day. Here, that would be Halloween and the day after."

"Los barriletes guían a los espíritus a visitar a los vivos."

I grab "spirits," "visit," and "living" out of that sentence and watch her raised hands lower slowly. She must mean that the kites help spirits visit the living. "They're so colorful, like giant kaleidoscopes," I say.

The picture of Solana's mother surfaces in my mind. "Solana," I say gently. "¿Tu mamá?" I hope she can guess what I'm asking. I wonder if she ever flew a kite to reach out to her mother's spirit.

"Ah," Solana smiles. "Mi mamá está aquí." She points to her heart.

We flip through a few more pages. "Hey, have you won any contests with these drawings? Any medals? These are *so* good."

She tilts her head, and I search my brain for a Spanish word that fits. Awards! "¿Premios?"

Solana shakes her head. "No, no, no. No muestro mis dibujos a nadie."

She doesn't show them to anyone? "Why not?"

Solana turns a couple of pages before answering in English, "I like colors. No premios. I put the colors to feel . . ." She touches her heart and opens her arms.

I try to hear through the words to the meaning. She likes drawing for fun, it sounds like. Just for the colors and for how it feels. For its own sake.

I can't imagine drawing like this and not showing people. She could totally win a contest.

"Aquí hay uno que dibujé en el avión." She points to another drawing. "On the airplane to here, I draw."

The colored chalk shows a girl with wings, flying in the sky. She wears the same dress and ribbon belt that Solana wore that first day. The girl looks small in the wide sky. I can't tell if she is flying away from something or toward something. It seems sad and miraculous at the same time. "Is this you?"

"Sí, soy yo, pero me inspiró Paula Nicho, una gran artista maya de Guatemala. Hizo una famosa pintura de una joven maya que volaba lejos de su casa."

I'm lost this time, but instead of trying to say it in English, Solana walks to the living room coffee table. She lifts a large book about Guatemala that I used to flip through.

She opens to a painting that's much like her drawing. A Mayan woman in her native outfit flies away from her village on wings. A dog below watches sadly, looking like he wants to go with her.

Solana taps a photograph of the artist. "Paula Nicho Cúmez."

I get it. Solana drew herself flying, and this artist inspired her.

Solana closes the sketchbook and holds it to her chest. A moment of silence follows. She doesn't show her drawings to anyone, but she showed them to me. "Gracias," I say, wishing I knew a bigger word, a longer sentence, that would tell her the whole feeling I have. I'm not even sure how I would describe it in English. But it's deep and warm, and for the first time, I feel like we're sisters. Even friends.

"Solana, I'm taking you to meet someone." I point out the window. "Conocer." All I remember is "to get to know."

"¿Conocer a alguien?"

I'm so glad she can read my mind right now. "Sí."

"Who?" she says in English.

"A computer man." I look to see if she understands.

"Un programador?"

"Yes, yes. A programmer. His name is Mr. MacLellan. Señor Mac. And he lives across the street."

"¿Vive en la calle?" She pulls in a sharp breath.

"No, no. Not *on* the street. *Across* the street. Over there," I point out the front window with my fork. "He made our mailbox light."

Her squint tells me I've lost *her* this time. I throw out some individual words. "Luz. Caja. Cartas." Light, box, letters.

Her features relax as understanding breaks over her face. "La luz en el buzón." After a last bite of cake, she says, "Very cool person." Her "very" comes out "bery," but I understand easily.

I lick the last of the icing off my fork. "Ready?" Only a few days ago I was sure I'd never be doing this. Now I can't imagine leaving her out.

28

"Why, you must be Solana!" Mr. Mac thumps his cane on the garage floor as if adding an exclamation point.

"Señor." Solana dips her head and makes a little bow.

"Well, bless my soul, aren't you the polite one! Name's MacLellan, but you can call me Mr. Mac."

"So very nice to meet you."

"Oh, pshaw, the pleasure's all mine, all mine," he says, waving a hand in the air. "Luz, this is a real treat, seeing you two." His eyes twinkle, as if he knew all along that I'd bring her eventually.

He turns to Solana. "Welcome to the garage! These are my scientist friends," he says, gesturing to his posters. He gives her a tour, pointing out the main areas—computers, workbench, tools—and then brings out Little Red. Soon Solana is zipping the car in loops and swerves around the driveway.

Meanwhile, I turn on the ancient Apple II+. I want to show her my Magic 8-Ball. I still think it's cool, even if it is simple.

The screen comes to life, its blocky green cursor blinking. I relive the thrill of running the code and having it work on the first try. Now I'll add Spanish.

"We saw robot brains at the club today," I say.

"Did they have motherboards, like those?" Mr. Mac points to some flat green boards leaning against each other on a shelf.

"No. We couldn't see inside. I guess we saw robot *heads*. They look like white blocks with screens on top. You can plug in sensors and motors. One kid is programming his in Scratch!"

"I knew Scratch would be the perfect next step, didn't I?" Mr. Mac says proudly.

"You totally did, Mr. Mac."

"I'm glad you brought Solana," he says in a half whisper.

"Yeah." I look down at the keyboard, a little embarrassed that I thought I didn't want her here.

"Mr. Mac?" I say. "Can I use your tablet for Google Translate? I want to make this 8-Ball bilingual." I bring up the translated phrases, add them to the opening PRINT line, and type "RUN." It looks right, so I motion Solana to come over.

She leans over my shoulder to read the screen.

YOU MAY APPROACH! ASK YOUR YES-NO QUESTION.

¡PUEDES ACERCARTE! HAZ TU PREGUNTA DE SÍ O NO.

Solana's eyes get big as Oreos.

"Go ahead. Type your question." I push back from the keyboard.

"¿Sabe español?"

"Sure, it knows Spanish," I say. In fact, I'm teasing. The computer doesn't know what the human types. It just waits for ENTER and then gives one of the answers.

Solana punches the fat brown keys, asking her question in Spanish.

`TOTALLY! ¡ES CIERTO!`

"Wow," she says in English.

"Let me show you the code."

I end the program and bring up the code. She sees the list of responses and reads them. `YES/SÍ`, `NO`, `LEANIN' TOWARD YES/PROBABLEMENTE`. When she gets to `TOTALLY!/¡ES CIERTO!`, she claps her hand to her head. "¡Comprendo! I understand."

Now she knows how it works.

"I have an idea," says Mr. Mac. "You could code that same Magic 8-Ball in Scratch. It would make a good first project, and you already know the concepts." He says this from his stool at the workbench.

"Yeah. But I want to do something new, Mr. Mac." I turn to Solana. "I need to learn Scratch," I explain. Her eyebrows furrow. I'm guessing she doesn't know what Scratch is. I guess I don't either.

"Come over to the laptop," says Mr. Mac. "I installed it yesterday."

Mr. Mac slides off the stool to stand up, but suddenly, there's a crash as his cane slips to the floor. He wobbles for a second, teetering on one leg. *He's going to fall!* I rush over, but he grabs the workbench, catching himself.

"I'm okay," he says. "I'm okay."

Solana fetches his cane and hands it to him, saying something that sounds worried.

"Are you really okay?" I ask. His hand is shaking again, too, but maybe he's rattled right now. After all, he almost nosedived into the concrete.

"Sure, sure. I've just been a little off recently. Not sleeping well. I'll be right as rain once I get a good sleep."

"If you say so, Mr. Mac." I'm not completely buying that.

"Let's look at Scratch, shall we?" Mr. Mac energizes his voice, trying to put us at ease, I think.

I follow him, watching to see that he's steady. Solana hovers around him like a guard in a basketball game, arms out at her sides. When he sits down at the laptop, we both relax.

"What are you learning in that intro class, Luz?" he asks, typing.

I can hardly remember. I try to picture Mr. Sung's room at the elementary school. "Oh, yeah. Today was the history of robots." I try to think of the most interesting part. "Leonardo da Vinci made a mechanical knight five hundred years ago. It could lift its sword."

"No kidding?" says Mr. Mac. "He must have used pulleys." Mr. Mac types a few keystrokes and sits back. "Here it is."

We're looking at a screen with blue bubbly blocks lining the left side, a large white field in the middle, and a little white square on the right with a smiling fox inside.

Solana and I pull up chairs.

"Welcome to Scratch."

The three of us crowd around the screen.

"In Scratch, these blocks are your commands. You drag and drop them into place," Mr. Mac says, dropping a blue block onto the white field.

"This is pretty fancy, Mr. Mac. We're using a mouse!"

"Yup, we're in the twenty-first century now."

Solana startles, sits up super straight, and points to the screen. She says something three times, and points with both hands now. What in the world?

"Bring over the tablet, Luz," Mr. Mac says.

Before I can even get up, Solana is grabbing the mouse and clicking on a globe in the upper left corner. She clicks "español" from a drop-down list, and all the blocks change from English to Spanish!

"You've used Scratch before?" I ask.

Solana nods emphatically. "Scratch," she says, but it sounds like "escrah-tch." I see why she didn't get what we were talking about before.

She reaches for the keyboard, and Mr. Mac moves to the side. In ten seconds, she makes a stack of command blocks. Then she pauses dramatically as the mouse hovers over a green flag.

"¿Listos? Ready?" she says.

One click, and the small square on the right comes to life. The fox darts around the screen. Speech bubbles make him say, "¡Hola!" and "Solana es mi amiga."

"Wow! Solana knows Scratch!" I shout.

"Well, I'll be," says Mr. Mac.

Where did you learn? I type into the translator.

My uncle runs an electronics store. He put Scratch on the demonstration computer, and I played with it.

Demonstration computer? She must mean something like a store model. "How great!"

When I left Guatemala, I was making a Mayan horoscope using the Tzolk'in, she types.

Tzolk'in? Not even Google knows what that is. It must be a Mayan word.

You put in your birthday, and it tells you your personality. And your Nahual—your day sign and animal guide.

"I have an animal guide?"

"Vuelvo enseguida," Solana says before racing across the street and disappearing inside our house.

I'm left blinking.

"Is she coming back?" Mr. Mac asks.

"I think so." I watch our front door to see if it opens again.

"You know, Luz," Mr. Mac says, "I'm no expert on sisters, but you two seem to be getting along. My two lights across the street?"

I have to nod, sheepish *again* at how wrong I was. Solana and I do have things in common. "I know her better now."

Our front door slams, and Solana runs down our steep driveway on her toes, carrying some kind of folder.

Still catching her breath, she huffs out a few words I understand. "Calendar" is one.

A birthday gift from my mother, she types.

Then she hands me the big, beautiful folder-card. The cover says ¡Feliz cumpleaños!, which I recognize as "Happy Birthday!" I open it up to see a ring of intricate symbols circling a kneeling figure on one side, and a long table of numbers on the other. The back shows each symbol next to its own paragraph.

"What a treasure this is," Mr. Mac says. "Thick paper and vibrant colors."

It's like nothing I've ever seen.

When is your birthday? she types.

"June ninth," I say.

She looks up the date on the table. **Your Nahual is the Jaguar, or Ix.** On the back, she reads a whole paragraph about the Jaguar, and she types in most of it.

Jaguars have strength and high energy. These people can be builders and makers unless they become angry. Traits: intelligent, courageous,

decisive, practical. Watch out, jaguars, for being too proud, eager for honor, and envious. Try to be more thankful.

"Hey, that does sound like me." I like the builders and makers part. Maybe the negatives are a little true, too. . . .

Not all the Nahuales are animals, but mine is a spider monkey, or B'atz. Solana types. **They like to entertain people.**

Yeah, that makes sense.

The Maya say each day has its own energy.

"And who's that guy in the middle?" I point.

He's a time carrier. He carries a whole year on his back. When his year ends, he hands time to the next carrier.

I never thought of time like that, I type.

They say it is like a relay race. The gods are runners, and time is the baton that one god passes to the next.

I picture runners at the Olympics, passing the metal baton to the next runner. **Do the Maya have the same months as we do?** I ask.

No, they have three calendar wheels that all work together. But my chart tells us which Nahuales to use.

"Handy," I say aloud. **So how were you programming this in Scratch?**

She deletes the darting fox program on the screen and starts a new one. She clicks two buttons to find a premade dragon and a forest background. With a few blocks, she makes the dragon say, "FIND YOUR BIRTHDAY" in a speech bubble, with a magic wand sound effect.

That must be as far as she got.

"What a good first Scratch project," Mr. Mac says. "You can do it together. Then anyone can type in their birthday and find out their . . . nawal, was it?"

"Nahual," Solana says, nodding.

"Let's make it!" I say.

Solana taps her finger on the paragraphs on her folder-card. She's right. We'll have to type in all that text. But with two of us, it'll go fast. "We can do it," I say. My brain grabs a Spanish phrase that means the same thing: "Sí, se puede."

"Try a few of the tutorials, Luz." Mr. Mac points to the screen and a little light bulb icon. "Click that. You'll catch on. It's tricky at first, but not as hard as putting socks on a rooster."

"Mr. Mac!" I laugh. "You must have made that one up!"

"Nope, my mama said it often. She also said, 'The more mistakes, the more you're learning.' And she was right. Decide how to frame up that Mayan horoscope, but then be ready to debug and start over if you need to."

I pull up a chair next to Solana. She shows me some simple blocks, and I try out the tutorials. We sketch a plan for our Nahual program on paper and then start coding. We toggle between Spanish and English labels, so we both know what the blocks say and do. Sometimes I drag the blocks; sometimes she does. Sometimes she clicks exactly the one I was thinking of. It's like we're in Mom's band, hearing the same melody. Thanks to coding, we've found a language we share.

We work until Mr. Mac's nighttime lights come on along his driveway. By then, we're not just trying out little groups of coding blocks, we're using a bunch of them together. Mr. Mac was right that my training in BASIC gave me useful concepts. Scratch uses the same patterns. And since Scratch can talk to the robots at school, I'll make my Showcase program in Scratch, like Trevor's.

Solana and I have just finished a section when she looks up, gasps, and says, "Qué intrincado es ese diseño."

All I get from that is "intricate," but I follow her gaze. She's marveling at Mr. Mac's screen. It isn't his tracker project. It's something different. And beautiful.

30

"What's that, Mr. Mac?"

His screen clears and a small fern sprouts baby ferns. And the baby ferns sprout more ferns until the screen shows one big fern made out of tiny ferns.

"That's amazing," I say. "Do it again."

Again the fern grows across the screen.

"It's a fractal," Mr. Mac says. "You see the self-similarity? Each part is the same shape as the whole. Here's another one."

This time a Y branches out to look like a tree. Each Y grows another Y, which grows another Y, until it fills the screen. Solana and I clonk heads as we both lean in to see the detail. Every twig is the same shape as the trunk.

"How does it work?" I ask.

"Basically, we repeat a pattern over and over," Mr. Mac says. "Some fractal art is breathtaking. Google it, and you'll see." He leans back and says, "Math is downright beautiful."

I realize I'm actually starting to believe that.

"My wife was a mathematician."

"¿Su esposa?" Solana asks.

"Your spouse?" I translate.

"Yes, here she is." Mr. Mac picks up a photo from the desk.

I never thought about *Mrs.* MacLellan before, though I've noticed that picture.

"Lovely woman, she was. And smart as a whip," he says.

"Like the ENIAC women?" I ask.

"A lot like them in ability; they were her science grandmothers, you might say. But there was no one like her."

Solana and I stay quiet as Mr. Mac looks into the space just beyond the photo. "On our first date, I took her onto my roof with a telescope. We looked at moon craters and located Jupiter. I thought I was teaching her something, but then she taught me the Drake equation!" He turns to us. "The Drake equation predicts how many intelligent civilizations might exist in the universe."

"Whoa, what a brainiac!"

"I proposed to her as soon as I could work up the nerve." Mr. Mac puts down the photo and comes out of his reverie. "I'm sorry, Solana," he says, and reaches for the tablet to translate the story.

"¡Qué romántico!" she says.

"My Nora wished more women would pursue science. She would have loved to meet you both."

Solana types a question. **How are fractals used?**

"Oh, yes, fractals! Fractals only exist in computers, not in nature. Not in pure forms, anyway. But they help us make digital models of natural processes, like bacteria growing. Or clouds forming. Luz, can you translate that?"

"Say it again?" I ask.

He repeats more slowly, and Solana reads along with my typing.

I get a little thrill thinking about clouds and math connecting. It's like my brain never let those two things talk to each other before. They seemed too different.

"I've wondered if God is a kind of fractal," Mr. Mac says, looking at his tree made of trees. "An idea that copied itself into a universe."

I try to picture a thought becoming an atom, becoming a solar system, becoming alive. I never thought of God that way before, like a piece of math that leads to everything. I chew my lip for a second. "I think of God as sort of like honey stirred into tea, dissolved into it all."

Solana nods and says, "Dios es la energía que sostiene todo." Typing, she shows me the screen.

"God is energy that sustains everything," I read aloud.

We all look at each other. Between her energy and my honey and Mr. Mac's math, it feels like we've hit upon something. Like we've opened three doors into a huge room. We all seem to breathe in sync.

We hang in a beat of silence, until Mr. Mac slowly pushes back from his desk.

"Chop wood, carry water," he says. To our questioning faces, he continues. "Part of inspiration is attending to the simple tasks of life. Even spiritualizing them. So I think it's time for me to sand some wood." He chuckles.

"Can we come over tomorrow?" I ask. "It'll be Saturday."

"Of course! Now, if the garage door is closed, I could be taking a nap. I never used to need naps. . . ." He shakes his head. "Otherwise, my garage is your garage."

We do a three-way high five, and Mr. Mac lowers the garage door behind us.

Back home in our room, Solana asks me, "¿Qué es 'eniac'?"

Oh, yeah. I mentioned that at Mr. Mac's without translating. I show her a web page about the ENIAC women and proudly pull out my poster.

"¿Lo podemos colgar?" She gestures to the blank wall.

"Hang it, you mean?" I squeeze her elbow. "Solana, I am so glad you said that."

We point at different spots in the room and decide to hang it over the bookshelf. With two step stools and some pushpins, we each tack up one side. Back on the floor, looking at the women who worked together to help in World War II, I can't help feeling lucky about Solana. This sister thing could be okay.

"We have much luck, Luz." Solana's English sentence startles me, partly because she's thinking about luck, too. "In Guatemala, we have la violencia."

Violence.

"Here, la seguridad."

Safety.

She picks up the tablet to say something more. **Scratch reminded me of home. While I played on the computer, my mom would drink coffee with my aunt. I didn't know about the danger then.**

"What danger?" I ask.

After a long pause, Solana types again. **When someone dies, you appreciate everyone more.**

I turn this over in my mind. She must mean her mother dying. But why was she talking about violence?

That's the thing about Solana. She *does* appreciate people. It's almost her superpower. Maybe this is why she talks to everyone so easily? She liked me the very first day, for no reason at all. Which is odd, when you think about it. Sweet, of course, but I don't like people for no reason. I mean, even my parents don't. They love each other—for reasons. They love me for reasons, too. And now I have reasons to like Solana. Good ones.

I'm glad you're here, I type.

We brush our teeth, and I climb up to the top bunk. Solana pulls out her sketchbook. I try not to seem nosy, but from up here, over her shoulder I see a fern fractal.

Lying back, my mind scrolls through the day. Fractals. Nahuales. Scratch. The bubble-shaped commands float behind my eyelids. Maybe I really *can* code a program that will wow Ms. Freeman and my parents and the whole Robotics Club. I fall asleep imagining all the possibilities.

31

My nose wakes up first. Dad and Mom are cooking!

I keep my eyes closed, snuggle deeper under the covers, and inhale. It's Saturday, so I can lie here a long time, just savoring the smells. Fried eggs with salt. Ripe plantains simmered in oil. Fresh cilantro, probably on top of black beans, and homemade corn tortillas. A full Guatemalan breakfast like my abuela made when we visited.

When my stomach growls, I jump off the top bunk. I'm excited to get to Mr. Mac's and code some more.

I dress quickly and run a comb through my hair.

Sure enough, all the food I imagined is there, steaming, on the table. We all sit down together, and it feels more like supper than breakfast. "It all smells so good," I say. Solana understands and makes a mm-hmm sound.

"What's everyone planning for today?" Mom says.

"Solana and I are coding a Mayan horoscope. Mr. Mac started teaching me Scratch, a computer language."

"You're really getting into computers," Dad says. He actually looks okay about it, but then adds, "I'm sorry I can't help you with that."

"That's okay. Mr. Mac is perfect. He used to work at Texas Instruments."

Dad dishes up some plantains before answering. "We're, um, lucky to have him as a neighbor." Now he purses his lips, like it's taking some effort to say this. Why is he always sad about what I do?

He looks to Solana. "¿Qué vas a hacer hoy?"

She says something that includes Mr. Mac's name, too. He nods and turns back to me. "Luz, make sure you don't trip on the driveway."

No way. He is NOT doing this again. It's true that I fell once on the driveway when I had crutches, but that was months ago. I throw my napkin down next to my plate. "Dad, I'm *always* careful on the driveway. And everywhere else! Stop talking about my injury all the time. I'm sick of it!"

Dad throws up his hands, and Mom pushes back from the table.

"Luz, why are you so angry these days?" Mom raises her voice. "Everything we say sets you off. Can't we have just one meal in peace?" She's not only frowning—she drops her knife and fork with a clatter. "We worked hard this morning to make this nice breakfast and now you . . ."

The next noise I hear is a thud, a squeal, and quiet crying. We all turn to look at Solana. Her blouse is covered in

160

black liquid, and the entire serving dish of black beans lies upside-down on the carpet.

Mom rubs her whole face with both hands and Dad lets out a groan. We're all frozen in a Misery Moment with everything wrong.

"I can get it," I say. I start picking up the dish, the serving spoon, and piles of beans. I dump the beans in the trash and come back with a damp dish towel. Solana's still crying. "It's just an accident," I say. "Accidente."

Finally, Mom and Dad unfreeze. Mom puts her arm around Solana, and Dad starts comforting her in soft Spanish.

Suddenly Solana's arms are up, flinging and pointing. She's shouting. Actually angry. I'm so stunned that I stop cleaning the floor and stare.

"What's she saying?" I ask.

"She can't understand why we have carpet under the dining table. In Guatemala, she had tile," Mom says, in a high tone that tells me even she's confused.

"But it's fine," I say. "It's almost clean already. And there's more on the stove."

"She's stressed, okay?" Dad shouts. "This has been hard for her! It's not even about the beans."

Now Solana's crying in a different way, head down on the table, arms wrapped around her head. *Lo siento, lo siento,* she's sobbing. I'm sorry. I'm sorry.

I remember her aunt's plan. The instructions on how to be helpful and make us like her. How could she think that spilling some beans on the floor means she's blown her chance?

"Solana, it's okay," I say in her ear. "It really is."

She sobs out something, and I look up for someone to translate.

Dad's face looks stricken, and he says slowly, "She says you're the real daughter, Luz, and she's a fake." He immediately tells her something that I hope is *No, you're awesome. You're not a fake at all. We love you.*

I want to hug her, but I don't want the dirty towel I'm holding to touch her hair.

Mom stands up, startling us all. Even Solana looks up at her. "Everyone. We need a reset."

What does she mean?

"Whatever you have planned for today can wait. We need to do something right now. Something fun, and something out of the house." She points to Dad. "Emilio, cancel that client meeting. Luz, you and Solana can go to Mr. MacLellan's later on." Her hands go to her hips, in a supermom pose. "Right now, we are going to see bluebonnets!"

Dad lets out a half laugh, but Mom might be on to something. A trip to the bluebonnets could *possibly* save the day. Trekking out to see spring wildflowers is a Texas tradition, and we do it each year. We have photos of me at every age sitting in a field of them. When I was five, we even got a butterfly in the picture. Bluebonnets aren't as big as the jungle flowers of Guatemala, but their stems, bristling with little blue blooms, are more than pretty. And a whole field of them, so thick you can't step between them—well, it'll just about make you cry. Solana's going to love it.

We clean up the remains of our failed breakfast, and Dad explains to Solana. I think she imagines a garden at first, but he's describing the fields of flowers along the roadsides that we hope to find.

Mom pulls out a soft-sided cooler, and she and I load it with bottled water, cheese sticks, and trail mix.

"Where have all our sun hats gone?" Dad calls from the hall closet. "Here they are! Diana, you're brilliant. I heard this is a prime weekend. The colors are supposed to be at their peak." He switches to Spanish to loop in Solana.

Solana's tears have dried, and she pitches in by feeding Zigzag and filling up her water dish.

As we work, the good mood in the room becomes almost visible, like confetti in the air. I can't believe that fifteen minutes ago we were all mad and miserable.

"Are we going to take sister pictures?" I say.

"Sure," Mom says.

I've seen a thousand photos of sisters sitting back to back in the bluebonnets, or siblings tiered shortest to tallest with the field of deep blue all around them. This time, that will be us.

In the car, Mom and Dad recall all the best bluebonnet fields and plan our route as we head generally east. Solana and I sit in the back seat looking out the windows.

"¡Tan plano!" she says, and motions with her hand as if smoothing a sheet. I get it. The ground *is* flat, which seems like an odd thing to be amazed about until I picture Guatemala. There, narrow roads twist along hillsides, and volcanoes frame the sky on all sides. Texas isn't lush, but it's got open skies and distant horizons, all right, at least here. *Don't forget the piney woods,* Mom always reminds me. She's from east Texas, where dense forests make the sky seem like bits of blue streamer snagged on the treetops.

We pull up to a huge field and climb out of the car. Solana clasps her hands and exclaims, "¡Ay! ¡Mira!"

The expanse of almost-purple blankets the land in every direction. Breathtaking.

"¿Por qué 'bonnets'?" Solana asks.

Dad answers in Spanish, and I bet he's telling her what he told me when I asked. The individual blooms resemble floppy sun bonnets worn by prairie women back in the day. But the whole flower looks more like an ice cream cone, with the blossoms sprouting all around the top of the stem. Not like a bonnet at all.

Mom throws me a hat, and I head into the field, stepping carefully so as not to trample the flowers. I love to get to the middle of a field. Instead of feeling lonely in the vastness, I feel part of it, like I'm a bluebonnet, too, born to soak up sun and wave in the wind.

From here, I see Mom pull out her phone to take pictures. She kneels down for close-ups. Dad and Solana walk together at the edge of the field, then wade deeper in.

I walk farther and farther out, part of me wishing I could walk beyond the field's edge, beyond the horizon, right up into the sky. I can see why Solana drew wings on herself and why Paula Nicho Cúmez, too, painted a flying woman. Something in us lifts, widens out. Something in us soars.

I turn back to see Mom still taking pictures. She's posing Dad and Solana, waving them closer together. Then Mom and Dad switch, and Dad clicks photos of Mom with Solana. For once I'm not jealous—though I do want that sister picture.

I step back toward my family, putting my feet in places flattened by people before me to leave as many perfectly standing bluebonnets as I can. Solana meets me in the field, and we choose a picture spot. "Back to back first!" I say, and Mom clicks her screen. Then we take a shot with our arms around each other and another with silly faces. We end with a four-person selfie, Dad's long arm holding the phone high.

We break out the snacks before heading home, kind of a handheld picnic. Why does a boring cheese stick taste so amazing when you're outside? Then comes the trail mix, my favorite kind, with cashews and nubs of chocolate.

"What a perfect day," Mom says as we drive out onto the main road.

Dad and I laugh. No doubt we're both remembering our disastrous morning. But, yeah, now it feels just right.

Solana is so quiet that I look over, and I'm surprised to see tears in her eyes. I throw her a look of concern, but she puts her finger to her lips, signaling me not to tell.

There are all kinds of tears. Happy, sad, stressed-out, mad. There's also the kind where you can't believe your luck and the kind where you are super relieved.

I don't know what kind Solana's are. Maybe more than one. She might be missing her mom, or she might be feeling like she belongs. Maybe lots of feelings are tangling up behind her eyes.

I hear her breathing even out, and her blinking goes back to normal. The highway hums beneath us, and Mom talks about a band at school; Dad talks about which trees are the best for the landscape he's designing. No one's pointing out ways for me to be safer. And no one's going out of their way to make sure Solana understands every word. She's less of a guest. We're all just ourselves, four different website pages that all link back to Home.

33

I can hardly sit still in Mr. Sung's class on Monday. "Today you'll work with a robot!" he says. He hands out the heads that I saw at the club, a white block with a screen and buttons on top. Even without a computer, the "brick," as he calls it, can be programmed to roll and turn—if we give it a body. We each build a skeleton structure with LEGO parts and plug in two motors that work as wheels.

Before the end of class, I can make it follow a zigzag line: turn left—go forward—turn right—go forward. I'm definitely using motors, I decide, for my Showcase project.

I pull open the heavy door to the lunchroom and almost bump into Skyler.

"Oh, hey," I say. I haven't talked to her since the day I switched from soccer to Robotics.

"Hey, Luz. It's been a minute."

"Yeah, I know." It's good to see her. "How's everything, Sky?"

She shrugs with one shoulder. "You know."

I nod.

"Actually, we're doing the dumbest drills at League. Your dad always had us scrimmage four on four. Way better." She shakes her head. "The League team doesn't have a lot of parents who know the game like he does."

"He does know his soccer," I say.

"It's not just that." She tugs on her backpack straps. Why does she look so sad?

I wait.

"I mean, you're so lucky. Not everyone has a dad like yours. Like, so devoted."

"Soccer is life, all right. Or *was* . . ."

"I mean devoted to *you*, Luz."

Oh! I'm still blinking as she waves and heads off. My mind floats for second as I think back to Dad as a coach and the easy closeness we used to have. Then I picture Skyler and her dad, but his face doesn't come into focus.

A rumble in my stomach brings me back to the cafeteria. Maybe I can talk to her later.

"Hi, y'all." I join Solana and Trevor at what is now our usual table.

Solana jumps up for a cross-table hug. "Luz!"

Trevor ignores his corn dog as he tries to do the capirucho yet again. "I get it one time in ten!" he says. "How do you do it, Solana?" To me he says, "She can do ten in a row."

I admit, it's impressive. "Hey, what projects have you done with the robots?" I ask.

"Oh, um . . . Hey, I got it! Are you seeing this?" He's finally caught it.

"It's a thing of beauty," I tease, allowing myself a little snarkiness.

"Projects . . ." He sets the toy aside. "Let's see." He flexes his fingers and shakes out his hands, like he's trying to get over a case of nerves. "Uh, I made the bot pick up a cube. I used the sensors to have it touch a wall and then turn. I made a launcher that throws stuff. Oh, and the best thing was the Ping-Pong ball catcher." It all comes out in a rush.

"Can you show me those at the club next time?"

"All of them?"

I guess that *would* take a while. "Maybe one each time?"

"Sure, sure. I can do that. I'm working on my Showcase project, too, though."

"Oh, of course. Duh." Oops! I should have known. Of course he can't spend his whole time teaching me.

Solana looks up at me. She's probably wondering what we're talking about. "Programas para el robot," I say. "So what's your Showcase project going to be?" I ask Trevor.

"That's top-secret!"

"Come on, just a hint," I tease.

He blushes a little. "Nope, not even a hint. Solana, make her stop." He nudges her, and she nudges him back.

I knew he liked her. Doesn't everyone?

As if on cue, the ELL girls walk by and Solana calls them over. "¡Alicia! ¡Lorena! ¡Mariana!"

The whole group talks on top of each other, with no one finishing a sentence before another one starts. It's like falling dominoes, with no end in sight. I did find out where they're all from. Alicia came from El Salvador last fall, Lorena from Mexico, and Mariana from Honduras.

Occasionally, one of them looks my way, like they might want to say something. But they always return to Solana, and Trevor is back to flipping the capirucho. *I* might as well be a crumb on this table. But maybe this is how Solana feels when I talk to Trevor without using Spanish?

While the gabfest goes on, I think about Scratch and the robot and Showcase possibilities. Do I want the robot to move to a location and complete a task? Or could the motors power a surface that spins or something? It can sense a wall, so maybe it could solve a maze? I need to know more about what the bot can do. And what Scratch can do. I watch Trevor with the capirucho. Maybe a game? I could program a screen game without using a robot. Nothing feels quite right yet. But something will come to me. Soon.

It better.

34

During the next month, I get lots of practice with the robots at the club. Soon I can program the projects Trevor talked about. Solana's right there with me, learning more about Scratch's visuals and animation. Coding takes us beyond English and Spanish. We both speak Scratch now.

The only problem is that I still haven't thought of a great Showcase project. I saw a robot play a xylophone online and another one play a guitar, but Ms. Freeman says I should come up with my own idea. She also said that the advanced class emphasizes programming, so a sumo bot that crashes into another bot isn't complicated enough for her. "That's more of a building challenge than a programming challenge," she says. I think they're pretty cool, but okay.

Now April is ending, and my time is running short.

"What's on your mind, kiddo?" Mom asks, picking up a flower. She's kneeling on a foam mat on the sidewalk because every spring she plants pansies around the mailbox. She turns the flower upside down to tap it out of its tray. I'm helping with the watering can.

I haven't told my parents about the Showcase. I was hoping to surprise them with a project so stupendous that they would forget about soccer and everything I can't do anymore. But maybe I should talk through some of it with Mom?

"You sure look thoughtful," she says, shielding her eyes with a garden-gloved hand.

"I can't think of a project."

"A project for school?"

"A Robotics project."

"Oh." She pokes holes in the dirt with her finger. "Is it part of Mr. Sung's class?"

"No. It's, um, extra. In fact . . ." I guess I can tell her. "It's for the May Showcase, a kind of science fair for all the robotics projects. I want to make something really special. If it's good enough, I might even get to take the advanced class in the fall."

"Wow, that sounds great, Luz." She sits back on her heels and looks up at me. "You're really taking off with programming. What kind of project does it need to be?"

"It's kind of hard to explain."

"Can I get some water here, please?"

I pour water into the holes in the dirt. "I need to code something in Scratch that also uses a robot."

"Sounds like a challenge." She plants a pansy and presses the soil firmly around it. She has a bunch more to go. She likes to plant every color she can find, and the garden store had plenty.

"I wanted to program a game, but . . ."

"Like a video game?"

"Yeah. I made a ball-and-paddle game, and Solana made a game where you catch falling fruit. But I want to try something harder."

"What about tic-tac-toe . . . or Mad Libs? You like those in real life."

I set down my watering can and think. What would it take to code the rules of tic-tac-toe? Lots of IF/ELSE's, but only nine squares to keep track of. Mad Libs would be easier. I could write scripts with missing words and have the screen replace blanks with user input. "Not bad, Mom. Those could work."

"Well, thanks. Can you water these over here?"

I pour, watching the water disappear into the dark soil, the rich kind with white fertilizer specks bought at the gardening store.

"Or a card game?" she says.

Lots of graphics and fifty-two cards to keep track of? "Too complicated, I think. And anyway, I need the robot to do something."

"What kinds of things can it do?"

"Well, it can roll and turn and stop. It can sense a wall and colors. It has sound files, so it can say words and play music. The thing I've practiced most is making it move."

"It's got the moves, huh?" She snaps her fingers and busts into a shoulder dance. *Geez, Mom, not out here in the open! Do parents take a class on how to embarrass their kids or something?* "Well, whatever you decide, you know we'll be cheering you on."

I almost drop the watering can as my heart unexpectedly lifts. Mom and Dad always literally cheered at my soccer games, whooping and hollering. That feeling—there was nothing like it. But Mom's saying they can still cheer me on. I think I believe her.

As I look into the treetops, and the wind flutters the leaves, an idea takes shape in my head. A game simple enough to code, movements that the robot can do. Suddenly, these seem more like a recipe than two disconnected things. Clouds + math. I wonder . . . I think through the steps of the game in my head. Yes. It has a pattern and an IF/ELSE part that repeats. It needs some lists of words and letters. It needs a graphic that updates itself as the game goes along. And like Mom said, we need cheering. I think it'll work. I think I can do it. I think I've found my project!

"Mom! I need to talk to Mr. Mac! I have an idea!"

"Oh! Well, okay, but come back and water these when I get them all planted. Deal?"

"Deal!" I say, setting down the watering can and starting across the street.

Solana will be excited to hear this. I won't interrupt her English lessons on YouTube, but I'll draw out flowcharts—one for the Scratch game and one for the robot's movements. Mr. Mac can help. Then I'll show her the whole plan.

"Thanks, Mom!" I call back. She really did help. More than she knows.

My feet feel like wings as I fast-walk to Mr. Mac's garage.

"Luz! How nice to see you."

"I have an idea for my Showcase program!" I hop right up on a stool to join him at the workbench. "It needs a couple of lists, plus a sprite who gives the user directions, a way to take user input, a way to compare the input with the lists . . . Are you all right, Mr. Mac?" He's having trouble holding the length of wood he's staining.

"Why do you ask?"

"Your hand is shaking again."

"It doesn't matter!"

His sharpness makes me flinch. I've never heard him talk that way. I hold my breath, waiting to see what will happen.

"I'm sorry, Luz." He sets the wood down and the stain rag, and sits back. "It's just that I've been so tired this morning. I'm making a giant Jenga game for my grandson, but the staining is slow going."

"Is that what those long blocks are?" I ask quietly, in case he's still upset.

"That's right."

"Wow." Each piece is big as my arm. "You always think of the coolest stuff."

"Can you fetch that wood-burner from the shelf under the bench there? When I bend down, I get a little dizzy."

"Sure I can." I'm still watchful, but Mr. Mac seems back to normal. He said he was tired, and dizzy, too. No wonder he's frustrated.

"Here you go." I hand him a plastic bin that seems to have a giant pen attached to a cord, plus some metal parts. "What will you do with it?"

"This stylus burns the wood. I'll write Connor's name on each block."

"He'll love that," I say.

"I'll just put this over here for now." He turns to set the bin on a counter behind him, but his hand trembles. The whole bin wobbles, and a *slam* echoes through the garage as the bin hits the floor. "Dagnabbit!"

I rush to pick it up and set it on the counter for him. "It doesn't look broken or anything," I offer.

His eyes go from fierce to soft, and his shoulders lower. In fact, he looks like he could cry.

"I do believe I'll sit down in my chair, Luz."

"Good idea, Mr. Mac."

Using his cane, he takes slow steps to the padded swivel chair in front of his main computer. As he sinks into the seat, he closes his eyes. Maybe he didn't sleep right last night.

"I'm glad you have an idea for your project, Luz. Very exciting."

I can tell he means it even though his voice is weak.

Footsteps slap the pavement in the street, and I turn to see Solana in motion. "Luz, I finish the lesson twelve!"

"High five!" I say, meeting her hand in the air. "And I thought of a project for the Showcase!"

"So . . . nice to . . . see you, Solana," Mr. Mac manages to say, breathing heavily.

I don't tell her what happened, but I will later. I'm starting to think Mr. Mac might be sick or something.

I turn to Solana and give her my main idea, then explain some of the parts. "The user makes a guess, and the computer compares that to a list. The robot says, "Uh-oh!" if they guess wrong. If they guess right, it says, "Good job!"

She must understand most of that because she nods, saying, "También, it needs to know how many guesses the user is already have," she says. Her English is getting good.

"You're right! It has to count the guesses. The program has to know when the user runs out. Plus, it has to make the picture change for each wrong guess." I'm so glad she thought of that.

Solana takes a longer look at Mr. Mac. He's usually jumped in with a science quote by now or a comment on a program. "Mr. Mac," she says. "You need some of the water?"

"No, I'm fine, Solana. Thank you, though." He sits up straighter and taps his cane on the ground. "Girls, I want to make you something. A little gift. Open that drawer there." He points to a workbench drawer just behind me.

Inside is a whole collection of drawer pulls. Round wooden knobs, glass spheres, metal bars, flat kitten faces, and more.

"Pick whichever one you want, and I'll make you a necklace out of it."

Ooh. This'll be sweet.

Solana examines a shiny blue one that seems to be made from glazed clay. I notice one with a compass rose. Then we both see it at the same time. A frosted glass heart with a deep red mini heart tucked inside. I'm thinking that I should let her have it when I see another one. We can both have one!

"Bring me that saw from the wall, Luz. And Solana? Find two ceiling fan pull chains in that box." He pantomimes and points, so she'll understand.

When she holds up two beaded chains, he says, "Just right."

He saws off the screw embedded in the back of each drawer pull. With epoxy glue, he attaches the chains to the hearts, and presents us with our necklaces. "To the best two youngsters a neighbor could ask for."

Now he looks like the Mr. Mac we know, smiling and generous. "Thank you Mr. Mac. I love it!" I say.

"¡Mil gracias! A thousand thanks!" Solana says, translating her own phrase.

I fasten Solana's necklace, and she fastens mine.

I'm eager to plan out my program, but Solana and I decide with silent looks and a couple of head gestures that we should let Mr. Mac rest. "We'll come back tomorrow," we tell him.

Back home, Dad and Mom meet us in the entryway with wide smiles.

"Mom tells me you figured out an important project, Luz." Dad holds up his hand for a high five.

"I sure did!" Our hands connect, and for a second, it's just like old times.

"And guess what? I just landed a big contract. Véliz Verde will be landscaping the new Arts Center!" He translates for Solana.

"¡Magnífico!" she says.

Mom leans into Dad, squeezing his waist. "We thought we'd celebrate with ice cream cones."

We pile in the car and drive to Antonio Joe's, the creamiest ice cream in north Texas.

"Get double scoops if you want!" Dad offers grandly, waving his wallet.

I order two scoops of Reese's 'n' Fudge. Solana tries one scoop of Raspberry Truffle and one Vanilla.

We sit outside on benches. "Let's get a picture!" Mom says. She manages to hold her ice cream and her phone, and we all smile. "I'll post this once I get this dripping under control," she laughs, licking quickly.

Solana startles when a police car goes by out on the main road, lights flashing. After that, I catch her looking up and down the street, her lips pressed hard together.

"You worried about something?" I ask.

She looks at me closely, trying to understand.

"Worried," I say clearly. "Preoccupied?"

"¿Preocupada? Sí, un poco."

So that's a yes.

She lowers her voice. "To here come la migra? Immigration?"

"You mean ICE? Immigration officers here? No, no." I don't, in fact, know if they would come to this shopping area. I guess they might, but not for her. She's becoming a naturalized citizen. Besides, don't they only arrest people who commit crimes?

Solana leans closer. "My friend at school, she say her brother, Rodrigo, was take. Very good man, deported. La migra come to his work and arrest him."

"Oh, how scary!" I imagine that scene and try to shake it from my head. "I hope he's okay. But Solana, immigration officers don't deport citizens or people with documents. You have documents." I lick the drips off my cone.

"Rodrigo, he has documents, too. The green card for working."

"What? That can't be right."

"Yes," she says. "Green card. And Luz . . ." Her face is losing its color. "He is killed."

"What? You mean murdered? For real? Who would kill him?"

Mom and Dad's heads turn in unison, and they stop licking their cones. Mom speaks first. "What's this about, girls?"

"Solana says that someone who was here legally got deported, and then . . ." I wince, not wanting to say it.

Solana goes on. "The gang in Guatemala. They wait for him at the airport, grab him, and shoot him."

This is the scariest thing I've ever heard. No wonder she's nervous.

"He escaped to the United States for safe. But the gang say, 'We get you someday.' And they did." Solana looks spooked, and my ice cream doesn't taste as sweet as before.

If he was snatched from work, his family didn't even say goodbye. A lump clogs my throat. And then he *dies*. It's too terrible.

"Girls," Dad says, taking a firm tone. "This is incredibly sad, absolutely horrible, but I don't want you to think it could happen to Solana." He catches Solana's gaze. "Solana, I promise the police won't take you. They're here to help you. Besides, you have a visa. Believe me, we have a whole folder of paperwork. Plus you'll be a citizen soon."

Her face is still tense, its curves all turned to lines.

"And your dad's been a citizen for over ten years," Mom adds.

They both go into Spanish to say all of this again.

Solana nods, but I can see that her breath hasn't slowed down. She's still troubled. And sad for her friend, of course. And Rodrigo. *I'm* sad, and I don't even know them.

"But how could this happen?" I ask. "Doesn't a green card mean that you have permission to be here?"

"Yes," Mom says. "It makes you a permanent resident. But green cards can be revoked sometimes."

A heat rises up through my body. "But Rodrigo needed to stay here. His life *depended* on it!" I throw the rest of my cone in the trash.

"I know, Luz." Dad looks into the treetops. "And we can't be sure he had a green card. He might have had 'authorized stay' status. Maybe he applied for asylum, but then got denied. They call reasons like Rodrigo's 'humanitarian,' and humanitarian reasons aren't always deemed important."

"Not important?" This makes no sense. My stomach hurts.

As we walk to the car, I wonder how many ELL kids have stories like this. Or if they worry, like Solana, that they could be next. Or their brothers. Or their parents.

37

I wake earlier than the whole house on Sunday. Above me, I hear the *thump-thump-thump* of squirrels chasing each other on the roof. A wave of thankfulness washes over me. It's no small thing to be safe, to be here. Solana stayed up late sketching something she didn't show me.

Quietly, I make my way to the dining room. I take out paper and pen, and sit down at the table. Time to map out this Showcase project.

I make a list of all the commands I'll need. I also draw the robot, starting with the brick I've used in school. Using two big motors and one small one, I should be able to make a humanoid shape that stands. By the time everyone else is eating breakfast, I'm ready to code.

After creamed eggs on toast, Mom says Solana and I can go to Mr. Mac's. We wear our necklaces and each work on our own projects until Mr. Mac speaks up.

"I need your help, girls."

"What for?" I ask.

"For the first demonstration of . . . drumroll please . . . the MacLellan Kid Tracker!"

Solana doesn't know about the tracker, so I take a second to explain in half Spanish, half English. She's on board. I turn back to Mr. Mac and say, "The Véliz demonstrators, at your service!"

Mr. Mac holds out a plastic dot the size of a thick nickel. "This is the tracking device. You go hide it somewhere, and we'll see if I can find it with the computer."

"It's so small," I say.

"It's a signal sender is all, so it can be small. This antenna brings the signal to the computer, and then the program here does all the work of locating the source of the signal. It's a little like how biologists track whales."

"Until where can it sense?" Solana asks.

"You mean how far?" Mr. Mac says. "It has a range of about twelve miles."

"Why need you a tracker?" she asks.

I didn't tell her that part.

"I have a grandson, Solana, whose name is Connor. He has autism. Sometimes he leaves home and gets lost."

"Autismo, sí. Él se perdió. Ya comprendo."

She understands.

"Connor did get seriously lost one day," he says. "Twenty-three terrible hours passed before we got him back."

He didn't mention this before. "That must have been horrible!"

"I didn't sleep a second all night." Mr. Mac shakes his head, remembering. "So now he'll have a tracker." His face brightens at this.

"We try it?" Solana says.

"Yes, try it!" Mr. Mac says. "You girls stick that one somewhere in the neighborhood, and then the computer will find it. Peel off that backing, and it'll stick to almost anything."

We carry the tracker out front and look for a place to put it. On a tree? On a mailbox? We walk toward our neighborhood jogging trail. I spot an empty cardboard egg carton lying in the grass. "Let's put it on that," I say. Solana agrees and peels off the backing. She presses it inside the lid of the carton, and we set it next to an overflowing trash can. I mash the tracker with my thumb to make sure it's stuck tight. Then we run back to Mr. Mac's.

"Can you see it yet?"

We gather around Mr. Mac's computer screen. "It's connecting to the maps now. Okay, now the signal should appear as a blinking dot."

Sure enough, a red dot shows up on a map of our neighborhood. I can see my own house's rooftop.

"It looks like it's on the trail. Is that right?"

"Yes!" we shout.

"Wait." Mr. Mac leans closer to the screen. "It's moving."

Solana and I look at each other. How could an egg carton be moving?

"I bet someone picked it up!" Mr. Mac says. "Or some-thing."

Now the dot makes a wide loop around the screen. Then it stays still. Then it takes off in a straight line before turning around and coming back.

"Wow, it's so accurate," I say. "We can see right where it is and where it's going."

"I think it's a dog, girls. See how it's going in a big spiral now? Haha! I didn't expect this good of a test! I think this tracker is history, though. Good thing I have several."

The dot stops, and I imagine the dog chewing on the egg carton.

"Qué buen trabajo," Solana says. "Good job."

"Thanks, Solana." Mr. Mac looks pleased. "Looks like I loaded the right wagon, eh? The program is almost done. I want to add one thing, though. Instead of a dot, I want it to show Connor's face."

I picture Connor's face wandering around the screen. "That'll be cute," I say.

I'm so glad to see Mr. Mac back to his usual self. His shaking is barely noticeable, and he's excited.

"Would each of you girls like to have a tracker? You can stick them on anything that you don't want to lose—maybe your backpack? Or your cat, Luz."

"Mmm." I think about this. "We could put it on her collar, but she might lose it. She wriggles out of her collar sometimes."

"Mira, Luz," Solana says, turning over her heart necklace. "Here." She sticks the tracker to the back of the heart. "You always find me."

"I love it," I say, doing the same with mine. "Now we're linked forever!"

She hugs me and does the two-cheek-kisses thing, and I actually like it. I kiss her back.

After school and every weekend, I code. I program both the robot and also the on-screen game. The game itself takes three sections—game flow, graphics changes, and word lists. Each day, I consult my paper map, then pull up to the keyboard.

Every Friday at the club, I build. Motors, sensors, beams, bushings. Two motors become legs, and sensors become hands for my robot. I choose sound effects and facial expressions for the brick's screen.

Solana is making a Scratch animation of her own. She designed a colorful quetzal that flies through the jungle, but she helps me, too, by making images. She's drawing robot parts, and a conveyor belt, using a paint editor.

We both wear our necklaces every day. I'm discovering that she's not just a sister; she's a friend.

We spend lunches with Trevor talking about coding. He still acts a little stilted around me, barely getting out his sentences sometimes, and is more relaxed with Solana. He's learning some Spanish to talk to her even more. *Don't be jealous*, I tell myself, but I admit, sometimes I stare too long when he's assembling, just to watch his eyes go from motor to sensor to keyboard. I have to remind myself, *You get to have a sister. A sister who people really like! That's pretty great.* He won't tell either of us what his project is.

When I can't get the game's loops quite right, I talk to Mr. Mac. As I'm describing problems to him, I hit upon answers.

May speeds by, and I remember the Mayan time runners. The days really do feel like strides in a race. My project is nearly done just as May hands the baton to June.

If all goes well, I'll be standing in the school library on Friday night, only three days from now, showing my project to Ms. Freeman in the Showcase.

> > >

One warm afternoon, I show up at Mr. Mac's with a heavy bag and a thrill corkscrewing through my whole body.

"Ah, Luz! Today's the day, right? The final test of your program?" he asks.

"Yup! I sure hope so, anyway." I'm feeling good about the game part, and I think I have the robot program done, too. In fact, Ms. Freeman let me bring the robot home overnight just so I can see if my Scratch program on Mr. Mac's computer can connect to the robot and run smoothly.

"Check this out." From the padded bag, I pull out the robot, careful not to snag its chunky arms and legs on the handles.

"What a beauty!" Mr. Mac says, his eyes shining. "May I?"

I hand it to him, and he looks over the white and gray plastic. He inspects the cables that connect the motors to the brick. He touches the small motor on the back that moves the hands. "Are the legs sturdy enough?"

"That's exactly the problem. At school, it fell down when it moved. I have some extra parts here. I think it needs bigger feet."

"I bet that will do the trick."

"Then I want to put in the last blocks of code for the game. I want the graphic at the end to be timed right with the robot's reaction. I think I have the Wait Block in the wrong place."

"Here comes Solana," Mr. Mac says. "Are those your friends?"

"What?" I look up from the workbench to see Solana, plus Alicia, Lorena, and Mariana crossing the street. Great. A triple threat.

"How did *they* get there?" I ask aloud. Last I heard, Solana was supposed to be at a thing after school. And this isn't Social Hour. I have work to do.

"It'll be a party," Mr. Mac says, though I can't tell if he's being sarcastic. *I* would be sarcastic if a gang of gabbing girls were about to invade my quiet workspace.

I know Solana loves to be friendly, but why did she bring friends *here*? This is our place, and she's ruining it. And she has me here; why does she need *them*? *Calm down, calm down, calm down,* I tell myself. *Try to be nice.*

"Good to see you, Solana!" Mr. Mac says. His smile looks real, but I wonder.

"This is Mr. Mac," Solana says to the girls.

"It's very nice to meet you," they all say in textbook English.

"Luz, is it not great? We completed early, and the girls carried me home in the car," Solana says.

"You guys are driving already?" I slip into a snideness that I haven't used in a while.

"Hi, Luz," Alicia says. "My mom brought us."

For some reason, her English startles me. It's like I didn't see a real girl in there before. I know it's silly, but she seems more alive or something. Maybe it's because she's not ditching me right now, like she did that one time. Or maybe it's been too convenient to ignore her. The story of Rodrigo flashes to mind; I need to be nicer. But this isn't the right moment to become her friend. I'm busy.

"You're all very welcome to my garage." Mr. Mac is a better host than I am. "Have a look around." It sounds rude, but I wish Mr. Mac were less nice right now. How will I get anything done with them here?

"Look! These are the old computers of Mr. Mac," Solana says. She sounds like a tour guide. "This one can answer any question."

"Any yes-no question," I put in.

"Luz made the Magic 8-Ball." Solana beams, like she's proud of me. But is she really? Maybe she's just proud to show off to her friends.

"You can show us?" Lorena asks.

I try not to exhale too loudly. "Sure." I insert a floppy disk in the Apple II+ and bring up the old program. Turns out, it feels good to click these chunky keys and remember my first "Hello World" program. When the familiar lines of code cascade down the screen, they feel like friends. More than these girls do, for sure.

I step away as Solana takes over the demonstration. The girls ask questions in turn, slipping into Spanish sometimes, but mostly keeping to English. It's kind of amazing how fluent they are. Monolingual me is impressed. As they laugh and ask the computer sillier and sillier questions—*Can you buy me a unicorn?*—I almost smile. But I still wish they weren't here.

"You can find their Nahuales, too," Mr. Mac says. "On your computer."

Mr. Mac! But I need to use this one! I'm coding in Scratch offline, which means the code isn't on the internet anywhere, just on this machine. *That* means that I can't work on any other computer. Now I'll have to wait.

39

The girls all find their Nahuales and debate over whether their personalities are anything like what it says.

"I am not dreamy!" Mariana says, shaking her head.

"Says the girl who writes poems on her math homework!" Lorena teases.

"Pero . . . you are creative, Mariana," Solana says, turning it into a compliment.

I try not to roll my eyes. I'd rather be *doing* something. Not talking.

"How old is this system of Nahual?" Alicia asks.

Solana opens a browser and gets the answer. "This site says three thousand years. But, amigas, the best program of all is Luz's game," Solana says. "She's making it for the Showcase. It has a robot, too!"

Her smile makes me want to forgive her. She's so sweet. She must honestly enjoy hanging with bunches of people. I see that. I just don't understand it.

"Did you show them your quetzal animation?" I ask.

"I did!" Solana clasps her hands. "On a computer in the school."

"It was beautiful!" Alicia says. "A jaguar jumped and everything!"

It's true. Solana made the quetzal fly around the jungle meeting animals, from tiny tree frogs to a sleek jaguar.

All three girls gush about it for so long that I sit down at the keyboard and bring up my game program. I move the Wait Block, and find a few other tweaks to make. Soon I'm ready to run a full test of the program.

Oh yeah, the robot feet! I dump the extra parts on the workbench and add longer beams.

Lorena watches carefully. "This robot is complicated. You make the feet bigger, right?"

"Yes," I say, glad that she's interested in the right thing. "It was falling over."

Everyone watches as I reattach both legs.

"That should do it," I say.

I stand the robot upright and click through some menus on the brick's screen to connect it to Mr. Mac's Wi-Fi.

I always pictured unveiling my project in front of Ms. Freeman, the Robotics Club, and my parents at the library on Friday, but I guess this is fine. A dress rehearsal. Okay.

"The game is basically Hangman, but in this version, you build a robot," I say.

"El ahorcado, pero build a robot," Solana explains.

"If you guess a letter right, a new part is added to the robot on the screen. If you guess wrong, this conveyor belt moves it closer to the trap door. Solana made all the graphics." I send her a smile. She did a great job.

I motion to the empty chair, and Solana sits at the computer. The girls gather around her. Seven blanks across the top of the screen tell her that the mystery word is seven letters long.

She guesses *T*, and startles as the real robot stomps its foot and says, "Uh-oh!"

"Cool," says Lorena.

Solana guesses *E*, and this time the robot raises a hand and says, "High five!" She taps two fingers to the robot's hand.

She guesses right again a few more times, but then *R* is not in the word, and neither is *L* or *M*. The on-screen robot comes right up to the trap door.

"You cannot guess more wrong!" Alicia says.

"What word is this?" Lorena says, wondering.

"Maybe *S*?" Solana says.

"No, wait!" Mariana squeals.

Together they come up with "pancake."

The screen robot jumps off the conveyor belt, completed. The real robot on the workbench erupts in a trumpet fanfare. It says, "Way to go!" and does a jerky dance.

A perfect test! A wave of relief floods my body, followed by a light-headed happiness.

"Congratulations, Luz," Mr. Mac says. "That was better than a parade on the Fourth of July."

"Do you think it's enough for Ms. Freeman?" I ask. "Do you think she'll let me into Robotics Two?"

"We can't know for sure," Mr. Mac says. "But you can be proud of this."

I can. I am.

"I'll call the game GrowBot and this guy CheerBot."

Mr. Mac gives me a thumbs-up.

"The last thing I have to do is save the program to this flash drive." I can't believe I'm finally at this moment.

"Luz!" I hear my mom's voice from across the street. "You forgot the litter box!"

Facepalm. I was in such a hurry after school that I skipped cleaning out Zigzag's box.

"We can play more?" Mariana asks.

"Yeah, sure," I say. "I'll be right back."

I walk fast across the street and climb the steep driveway, good leg first. It seems incredible that my Showcase project is done. Actually done. Weeks of coding and testing, building and redesigning—all worth it.

Zigzag meets me at the door, and I've never cleaned a litter box in a happier mood.

I drop the poop-baggie into the trash and wash my hands at the kitchen sink as Dad wanders in from his office down the hall. "Dad, I did it! I finished my project!"

"That's great, Luz," he says into the fridge.

"It's more than great. I can't wait to show it to you!"

"Well, I can't wait to see it." He's still too calm.

"You know how I've been learning to code?"

"Over with Mr. Mac," he says, pouring himself some iced tea.

"Yes! Well, now I've coded a whole game. You can play it at the Showcase. Don't forget, it's Friday night."

"Friday night?" He takes a swig of his tea. "I was planning to take Solana to la panadería that night, the Guatemalan bakery. They're doing marimba concerts on the patio. Should I postpone it?"

"Of course you should postpone it! You can take her there anytime. You're always with her anyway."

He frowns. "Luz, that's not true."

I want to tell him it *is* true. He's *so* big on helping her. Telling her that she'll learn English like he did. Walking her around so that she learns the neighborhood. Setting up video calls with her aunt back in Guatemala. He's with her. All. The. Time.

But instead of saying any of that, I focus on what I want him to know.

"This Showcase is important, Dad. I've been working for it all spring. Do you realize that if my code is good enough, Ms. Freeman will let me take her advanced class? I'm trying to be *that* good. You have to come. You have to come see me win. Like before."

"What do you mean, 'like before'?" He sets down his tea, pushes up his glasses, and looks at me.

I squirm. I guess I've never said it out loud. "I miss you cheering for me. At soccer games."

His shoulders slump. "I miss that, too, Luz."

I can see that he's been sad about this whole thing, too. "I know there hasn't exactly been any reason to cheer, but there is now. On Friday. Please come, Dad."

"I'll be there," he says. "Count on it."

I leave the house with a bounce in my step. Dad's gonna come! He'll be there to see my code and how much I've learned. Mom, too. *"That's our Luz!"* I can hear it already.

Over at the garage, everyone is clustering around Mr. Mac's giant Jenga game. This is good news. I can save my new code on my flash drive and put the robot away. But somehow the room is too quiet. I don't hear the whir of the computer's fan.

In a few quick steps, I'm at the computer. A blank screen greets me instead of the game.

"Did you turn off the computer?" I ask the group.

Solana turns from the Jenga game. "Computer off? Yes, off."

"No off!" I sigh. "I needed to save the program first. And move it to this . . . Oh, never mind. I'm sure it did an auto-save."

I push the power button and pace. I can't sit. I'm too worried that my new tweaks to the program will be gone. But I really think it auto-saves pretty often. At least I remember what the changes were. Mainly the Wait Block.

Finally I can log in and bring up the file.

FILE NOT FOUND

What? How could it not be found? "Mr. Mac!"

He rolls over on his office chair. When he sees the error, he says, "Did you change the name of the file?"

"No, it's the same as before."

"Was the computer shut down properly, or did someone just press the power button?"

"Solana! Did you 'shut down' or just 'off'?"

She's squinting, so I'm not sure she understands the question. She's turned off computers plenty of times, though. She should know if she did it right. She finishes her Jenga turn, pulling a piece right out of the middle.

"*Yes.* Shut down," she says, finally.

Thank goodness.

"Some problem?" Solana asks, her eyebrows knitting in concern.

"Yes, a problem!" I push away from the desk with my fists.

Mr. Mac scoots in front of the keyboard.

"Have you found it, Mr. Mac?"

"I'm trying, Luz. My fingers don't type as fast as they used to. I'm going slower to be more accurate."

"Okay, I'm sorry," I say, tensing with worry. I stand up and pace behind him.

"Oh, dear," Mr. Mac says quietly.

"What?" I ask, stopping in my tracks.

"I'm afraid . . ." His voice trails off. "It looks like a virus, Luz. It's erased all the files."

"What? How did this happen? How could this . . . Solana, what did you do?"

Solana leaves her stool at the workbench to see the screen. "What happened?" she asks.

"What *happened*? We don't know! But you were the last one to touch it."

"I shut down," she says. "I shut down." Distress clouds her face.

"Was there anything unusual on the screen, dear?" Mr. Mac asks gently. "Did you see an internet screen?"

"Yes, internet. And a box to save space. But then shut-down."

"Ah," says Mr. Mac. "That box was probably fake. It's not your fault. They lied to you, Solana."

I shut my eyes tight, trying to will the whole thing away. To no one and everyone, I say, "There's no way I can code this all over again. The Showcase is in three days, and this took me *weeks*."

Solana tries to put an arm on my shoulder, but I shrug it off.

"You don't understand! This was everything." Tears start, but I blink them away. I don't want to cry in front of the girls. They probably don't understand what's happening.

"Mr. Mac, what if I took three days off from school and spent them here coding? My parents will hate it, but this is an emergency. I *have* to recode this. I have to be at the Showcase!"

Mr. Mac's face falls. "I'm so sorry, Luz. I was going to tell you girls today. I have to be out of town for a few days. My daughter has an evaluation lined up for me with some doctor in the city. It took a long while to get the appointment. . . ." He trails off.

"This can't be happening." My voice comes out as a wail. The girls are staring at me now.

Solana looks from me to them and back again. I guess I'm embarrassing her. She comes closer and says quietly, "I help with a new program."

I step away. "No. That won't work. We have no time!"

"Maybe you play Jenga?"

"Jenga!" Does she have no concept of what she has done? What I've lost? Not just the program, but the Showcase and impressing Ms. Freeman and getting into the advanced class and Mom and Dad taking a picture and all of it. "How can you say *Jenga*?"

"My friends, they are scared now." Solana's face is full of concern.

How can she worry more about them than me? "They'll be fine, Solana, but I won't. My project is gone. Gone!"

I walk back and forth, like I'm trapped in a never-ending loop.

"Luz," Solana tries. "I am sad."

I'm sure she's sad, but sad doesn't help. Sad can't bring it back. "You destroyed it. You messed up my only chance," I say bitterly. "Why did you even leave Guatemala? Did you come here just to ruin my life?"

The tears start to flow. I want to go home. Curl up in a corner and sob. But thanks to Solana, I don't even have a room of my own to cry in.

I stalk out of the garage and run down the street. Run. I pump my legs as fast as I ever have in my life. I pound the pavement with every stride. If my knee crumbles to bits, I don't care. My knee is nothing compared to my heart right now. It's nothing compared to the program deleted out of existence. A messed-up leg would only show what's true all over again, that I'm nothing but a broken girl.

41

Even though my breath comes rough and ragged, I keep running. I take one turn and then another, not caring where the sidewalks lead. My ears fill with the sounds of blood and breath. I vaguely register that the day is warm, my jeans too hot.

Finally I slow down, first to a trot, then to a walk. My knee hasn't wobbled at all, but both legs feel quivery. I'm out of shape.

Though our park is almost a mile away, that's where I've ended up. I cross the parking lot, and the duck pond comes into view, and beyond that, the playground. Kids swarm the playground, so I walk to the pond instead, to be alone.

The shadows deepen under the cypress trees that line the water's edge. I step around the tree's knees, roots that stick straight up like gnarled arms cut off at the elbows. Now my own knee starts to throb. The pain makes me tear up again, not because it hurts, but because I can't get past it. I can't seem to leave the injury behind. It's always there, reminding me that I can't be special, that I can't be a star, that no one will ever cheer for me now.

A couple of ducks paddle toward me, probably expecting some bread chunks. "I've got nothing for you," I say aloud. Nothing for anyone.

The garage scene replays in my head. I see Mr. Mac's defeated expression, his hand propping up his forehead. I see the girls and their wide, frightened eyes. And I see Solana. Her face stricken with shock as I yelled and shouted and yelled some more.

The exact words come back to me. *Why did you even leave Guatemala? Did you come here just to ruin my life?*

My head drops. I know the computer virus was an accident. I even know that Solana is nothing but good to everyone. Unlike me.

I kick the dirt and look out over the water.

When did I become this person who yells so much? And why does everything I do end up in pieces? Bone: blown up. Code: blown away. Mr. Mac said to build a self. Well, I built one, and now look. It's a file not found.

A jogger goes by behind me. Squirrels chase each other up a tree trunk. Everyone seems to know who they are and what to do, especially Solana. Except for me.

I think of hanging the ENIAC poster on our wall and coding in the club at school. I remember her first days when we spoke through Google Translate. I picture her laughing at lunch. Laughing so readily, and letting everyone try the capirucho.

She came here determined to like people, determined to love my parents, determined to love me. I don't think she can now. Not after what I said. I wish she had less English. Now that she knows so much, I can't pretend that she didn't understand my worst words, my ugliest sentences.

I pull off my heart necklace. I don't deserve it. Solana doesn't want to be connected to me. I raise my arm to throw it in the lake.

But something stops me. Something my real heart can't let go of. Maybe it's that Mr. Mac gave it to us. Maybe it's that I want to love her even if she can't love me back anymore.

The fish don't want this in their lake, anyway, I tell myself, and stuff the heart in my pocket.

The water lies still and serene. The light has shifted from bright to muted. It's getting late. Probably dinnertime.

I walk around the lake, letting the edges of my shoes collect ridges of mud. When I've made a full circuit back to where I started, I stall. There's nothing to do but start home. Trudge back under a graying sky. But I hate the thought of facing Solana. And my parents. I'll have to apologize, of course. And I will. But it won't even matter because Solana won't trust me now, and my parents will be baffled. Mr. Mac probably won't forgive me for making a scene in his garage. I've disappointed everyone I care about.

My whole body feels wrung out like a rag. I lift a heavy foot onto the pavement and start the long walk home.

Instead of walking back the crooked way I came, I set out on the most efficient route. It takes me past the YMCA and a familiar stretch of grass—the soccer field I played on as a five- and six-year-old. I pause on the sidewalk, taking in the metal goalposts, newly painted, and the one park bench where parents clustered. The field looks small, much smaller than it did back then. I don't exactly plan to walk on the field, but I find myself in the middle, ankle-deep in Bermuda grass. In the fast-fading light, I wonder who I'd be if I'd never played soccer at all.

"Is that you, Luz?"

A shadow calls to me from the sidewalk, but I can't place the voice. Walking over, I try to make out their features. The main thing I see is a ball propped on this person's hip.

"I thought that was you."

It's Skyler.

"Hey, Sky. I didn't know you lived around here."

"Over there." She points in the opposite direction of my house. "What are you doing out here, Luz?"

"Oh, I . . . took a walk. You?" I'd rather get her talking than try to explain my complicated story.

"I was just swimming at the Y."

Only now do I notice her wet hair.

"Why the ball, then?" I nod at the soccer ball.

"Waiting for my sister. I thought I'd come out here and play around. It's their ball." She means the Y's, I guess. "You know, I always wanted to learn that spin you used to do. What is it called?"

"The Maradona spin?"

"Yeah. You faked out so many defenders with that. Can you show me?"

I haven't done that move in eight, maybe nine months, and the truth is, I should get home. "It's kind of late," I say.

"Just a couple times? I've tried watching videos, but they go too fast. You could teach me in five minutes."

It feels good to be asked. And it wouldn't take long. "I guess I have five minutes," I tell her, smiling.

She drops the ball, and I toe it over. The exact amount of hardness versus give in the ball's surface feels familiar. This one's not over-inflated, either. Just right.

"First, put the sole of your foot on top of the ball," I say. "Then pull it backward. See how it's going toward my back foot?"

She watches carefully.

"Now, as you pull it backward, you turn your back toward the defender. Your back foot can now pull the ball toward you again." I demonstrate twice, my body remembering exactly what to do. "It's also called the Roulette because your body spins as you switch feet."

"Do it again?"

I show her once more and then pass her the ball. "I'll be the defender." I station myself a little in front of her. She jogs toward me with the ball and almost does it. "You can also think of it as stopping the ball with that first foot. Once you have that down, work up to pulling it toward you."

She walks backward to gain some distance, then jogs toward me again. Her spin is awkward, but she's closer this time. The third time, she's got it.

"There! All you need is practice."

"Thanks! This will be great on the field." She practices a few more times before looking up. "Hey, so I noticed that you stopped coming to Athletic Hour."

"Yeah, I'm in Robotics now."

"That's different. It sounds . . . mathy."

"It's been cool, honestly." A pang in my chest reminds me that my best program is gone now. "I'm going to take it next year, too."

She nods. "If you ever want to come out to a game, it would still be fun to see you in the stands."

"Thanks. Have y'all been winning?" I've completely lost track.

"Not as much as I want." She laughs. "I just hope I'm good enough to get on the high school team in a couple of years."

"You totally will," I tell her. "With that spin? You're set."

Then I remember her comment about Dad, back in the cafeteria. Should I bring it up? She's smiling like her world is perfect, but I bet I look that way, too.

I let my gaze fall to the grass. "Hey, I wondered . . . remember when you talked about my dad? How he was a good coach and all? I hope, you know, that things are okay at your house."

Her eyes connect to mine and go sad. "He moved out."

"Oh, Sky, that's . . ."

"It's okay. Thanks for asking." She pops the soccer ball up from the ground using her toes and catches it in her hands. "No, I guess it's not okay. Honestly, it stinks, and I'm mad at him." She takes a deep breath and huffs it out.

I laugh softly. "Can you believe I've been mad at my dad, too?"

"No way."

"Yes way."

Skyler shakes her head. "I always thought your dad was the perfect dad."

I think of Skyler's healthy knees, Solana's friendliness, and me walking without a cane now. All looking fine outside, all carrying secrets. And Dad with the hugest secret of all—Solana herself. "My dad's got his issues, I promise. But he's working on them."

"Well, that's *something*." She spins the ball in her hands. "Grown-ups don't know as much as they want us to think they do. Did that make sense?"

"Definitely." I give a short laugh, and she smiles.

"You have to go now, huh?"

"Yeah, I better." I wish I could stay, but it's time. "Good luck with everything, Skyler. Especially that spin. You'll be the defender to beat, for sure."

As she walks back to the Y, I'm surprised that I'm not sad as I think of future games she'll play. I'm actually glad for her. And I have my own stuff to look forward to. Okay, not the Showcase anymore, and not Robotics 2, but coding something new, reconfiguring the robot. I've learned a lot, and that feels good. Even with the program erased, I have the commands in my head.

I thought everything depended on the Showcase, but maybe everything depends on me—not the yelling, whining me, but the self I'm creating. Maybe I *can* be "Luz in the world," like Mr. Mac said all those weeks ago. Not a broken girl, not a file not found. I can be a light.

Turning toward home, I set out. The tough thing now will be apologizing. And not only to Solana and Mr. Mac. The ELL girls, too. I wasn't considerate of them at all. Maybe at school? I'm sure they're home by now.

I just hope they all, especially Solana, will *let* me apologize. It could be that everyone's so mad at me that I can't fix this with I'm sorries. Again my terrible words to Solana boom in my head. Unkind. Unfair. Untake-backable. I'll just have to try.

43

As I turn onto our street, any courage I gained during my walk evaporates. Just seeing my house and Mr. Mac's house facing each other makes my stomach seize. What does Mr. Mac think of me now? His closed garage seems like a message. *Go away.*

Both houses are quiet, their yards empty. But in front of my house, a black SUV is parked. Its tall tires and dark windows look menacing. Who could that be? Are they visiting us or a neighbor?

As I get closer, I can make out a sticker on the side— some sort of seal. In a few more steps, the writing curved around the seal becomes clear: Immigration and Customs Enforcement. ICE. My stomach drops. I think of Solana's story of Rodrigo, the man who was sent back to Guatemala. Killed the day he arrived.

What are they doing here? Is Solana in trouble? Is *Dad* in trouble? But they both have all their documents. Then again, Rodrigo had a green card, so he was here legally, too. My heart races as I dash up the driveway, favoring my good leg. They *cannot* take Dad or Solana. No way, no way, no way. I will chain myself to their tires. I will tie the three of us together so they have to lift us, all or none.

"Dad! Solana!" I burst through the door, ready to tackle an ICE agent.

"Luz! Thank God! We were so worried!" Mom smothers me in a hug, and Dad piles on. It's our three-way hug, and I'm happy to be squished between them, barely able to breathe. I savor this moment before they find out what I've done.

"We didn't know where you were! Is Solana with you?" Mom asks.

"Wait, is ICE here to deport her?" I look to Mom and feel my bottom lip already quivering. "Or Dad?"

"What? No, no, no. The immigration officers are doing a survey," Mom says.

I'm so confused.

Mom and Dad lead me to the living room, where two men in suits stand up.

"Nice to meet you, Luz," one of them says with a nod.

I release a huge breath. "They're not taking anyone away?"

"No, not at all," says Dad. "No one's going anywhere."

A suit man says, "We're not the kind of agents who arrest people. We're here to ask about how the immigration process is going."

I guess that's why he's wearing dress clothes instead of a uniform.

"So Mr. Véliz, how long did it take for Solana's visa to come through?" says one.

"But where's Solana?" I interrupt.

"We thought she was at Mr. MacLellan's, or with you," Mom says.

"No. I . . . I ran off on my own." My voice gets softer as I end the sentence.

"Excuse me, sirs," Dad says to the men. He turns to me. "Mr. MacLellan called to say that you took off—without saying where you were going." He pauses to frown at me. "But he also said Solana was coming home after her friends left. A mom was picking up three girls and taking them home? Is that right?"

"I don't know," I say. "I left before they did."

"So you left," Mom clarifies, "and then the girls. So Solana left last?"

"I guess so." I'm getting nervous again. "Unless she's still over at Mr. Mac's."

"When she didn't show up here, we figured she found you, and you two were together," Mom says.

"We, um, had a fight," I say.

"What do you mean?" Mom says.

"I kind of yelled at her." I bite my lip.

"Oh, Luz. You didn't."

"I did." The disappointment on her face twists the guilt in my stomach.

"Let's set that aside for now," Dad says. "Go check through the window. See if you can see her at Mr. MacLellan's."

"The garage is closed," I say.

"Well, check again." Dad's voice comes out loud.

I hurry to the door. From there, I can see the closed garage door and the deserted street. And Mr. Mac's car isn't in the driveway. "I don't see her!" I call out.

"I'm calling Mr. MacLellan," Mom says, but she soon drops her phone to her side. "No answer," she tells us. "I left a message."

"Why wouldn't she come right home?" Dad says. He starts to pace.

"Maybe we should come back another time?" one of the suits says.

"Oh! Yes. I'm sorry," says Dad. "We seem to have a situation here."

"No problem, sir. We'll reschedule. I'm sure she'll turn up. Might have gone with her friends."

"Thanks," Mom says with a weak smile. "We'll look into that."

The agents file out, and I don't even say goodbye. I'm too worried. But she's probably fine, I reason. She's older than I am, and she does know the neighborhood. Suddenly, I sense a huge emptiness in the house, in the space where she should be. I can't imagine life without her. I don't care about the computer program or the advanced class or even my parents clapping for me. I want her back. I want her kisses on the cheek and her soft smile and her thick haircut to match mine.

I want my sister.

As the ICE SUV drives off, with its black tinted windows and official seal, it hits me. "I know what happened!" I shout.

My pacing parents look up.

"She got scared by the truck. The SUV from Immigration. Just like me. She thought ICE was going to send her back to Guatemala, so she ran away."

"But we would never let that happen," Mom says.

"And she's about to be a naturalized citizen. Doesn't she know she's safe?" Dad shakes his head and starts pacing again.

"Luz could be right, though," Mom says. "Especially considering her mother—"

"Diana, don't even mention that."

"Mention what?" I ask.

"We promised not to speak about it," Dad says through clenched teeth. "It's too much for her." He gives Mom a significant look.

"If this is about Solana, I deserve to know," I say. "It could help us find her."

Dad walks three steps away and walks back. "It's up to you," he says to Mom.

She takes a deep breath. "Okay, Luz. We didn't want to scare you. Guatemala's a wonderful country. So many lovely people. So much beauty."

"Mom, I know. We've been there."

"Yes, well . . . this is hard, Luz."

Dad takes up the task. "There are gangs. Drug gangs. They have a lot of money and a lot of power. They even target kids, recruit them."

"You mean kids join the gangs? Can't they say no?" I ask.

"That's the thing," Mom says. "The gangs threaten the kids and their families, too. Sometimes you're forced to join or . . ."

"Or be killed," Dad finishes.

My head hurts. It's hard to believe people would be so cruel. "But what does this have to do with Solana? Was she in a gang?"

"No, but . . ." Dad breaks off.

"Here, let's sit for a second," Mom says, sinking into the couch.

We all sit, and I almost cry, looking at Solana's sandals by the door.

"We never told you how Solana's mother died," Mom starts. "We aren't sure how she got involved—"

"Maybe she owed the gang money, or maybe she wouldn't marry one of them," Dad puts in.

"We don't know for sure. But she was shot in front of her house, Luz."

"With Solana inside," Dad says gravely.

"They tried to break into the house, but thank God some neighbors came out, and they left." Mom pauses. "Are you okay?

"Yeah," I say, though I'm a little stunned. I never imagined that Solana—sweet, sunny Solana—had come through such tragedy.

Dad takes over. "Well, the gang threatened to come for Solana. Maybe they wanted more revenge or to kidnap her or—" Mom reaches out and squeezes his hand. There's something worse they're not telling me. "In any case, it wasn't safe to stay there. Her aunt and uncle tracked me down here in the US, hoping that I would bring her here, to safety."

Several things make more sense now. The story of Rodrigo's death hit Solana hard, but now I see why it scared her so much. And now I see why she's so close to her friends. One of them at least, Rodrigo's sister, understands Solana's situation better than most people. They all understand better than I did.

I push the horror of her mother's murder to the side for now. I have to focus. "That ICE seal scared her, I just know it," I say. "Especially if she thinks a gang will get her if she goes back. We've got to find her."

Dad pulls out his phone. "I'm calling the police right now. She can't have gone far. She's on foot, so she has to be within a few miles."

"Unless she got into a car with a stranger. . . ." Mom's face goes white.

"Diana, don't think like that. She's smart. She wouldn't do that. Luz is right. She got spooked, and she ran. Let's see what the police can tell us."

"Of course," Mom says. "I'll call the neighbors. Someone may have seen her. And I'll see if someone can get me in touch with one of the friends she was with."

As Mom and Dad click their phones, I find I can't sit still. I want to do something, too. Zigzag rubs my shin, and I pick her up. I bury my face in her fur, hugging her gently. All I can think is *Solana, where are you?*

I walk back and forth in front of the window that looks out onto the street. I keep thinking I'll see her bounding up the driveway. Any minute, she'll appear on the sidewalk. But she doesn't appear, and the sky is turning from gray to purple. How long until dark?

I try to think of places she might be. The park? School?

A green light glows on the mailbox, meaning we have mail. I may as well go get it. But as I head to the door, I see a stack of envelopes and a magazine on the bookshelf near the door. "Did y'all already get the mail?" I call out. My parents, each on a different phone call, don't answer. Was that mail there this morning? No, it wasn't. That means it's today's. That means something besides mail is in our mailbox.

Good leg first, I step down the driveway toward the green light on the mailbox. Could it be a note from Solana? I shake my head. If she ran off, she probably didn't stop to write a letter.

I open the mailbox and there's Little Red, with a white envelope in its tray. I pull out the car and lift out the bulky envelope. A single piece of tape holds it closed. Right there in the street, I open it. Inside is a note—and a garage door opener.

> Dear Luz and Solana,
>
> I hope Little Red brought this to you safely.
>
> I need to tell you something that is hard to say. I've put it off because it is not happy news. I wanted to tell you today, but when your friends came, I knew I would have to find another way. This note will have to do.

I've been diagnosed with Parkinson's disease. That's the reason I'm tired, shaking, a little grumpy, and losing my balance. The disease damages nerve cells in the brain. It gets worse over time. While there is no cure, medicine helps. I don't want to "pour the milk until I've opened the carton," but if all goes well, my hand won't shake as much after some treatment. And to be clear, I'm not dying. Not yet! In fact, I'm still creating myself. Remember—not discovered, but created!

I'm going to a special doctor downtown, so I'm staying with my daughter and Connor for a couple of days. I'm bringing the giant Jenga to Connor. He'll help me finish it.

Luz, I'm so sad that your program file was erased by the computer virus. I'm afraid my machines aren't as secure as they should be. I feel responsible. If I can think of any way to help, I will.

Solana, don't feel bad. As I said, it wasn't your fault. I'm so glad you brought your friends today. My garage has rarely seen such a lively bunch!

Please use the garage door opener to work on any projects you like. My garage is all yours.

Just make sure you close it when you leave. And bring Little Red back to his shelf—thanks.

See you soon, and thanks for being my lights across the street,

Mr. Mac

The garage door opener goes heavy in my hand. Parkinson's disease. No wonder.

It's hard to believe that only an hour ago, I thought my program was the most important thing in my life. When I think of disease and deportation and Solana missing, I realize that people are what's important. Mr. Mac and Solana and Mom and Dad, even the ELL girls. They matter. Just for who they are.

And maybe that means I matter, too. Not for any prize I might win or program I might make, but just for me.

I refold the letter and put it in the envelope. My head clears, and I know what to do. I know how to find Solana.

I aim the garage door opener across the street and press the button. Mr. Mac's garage door clatters up as I close the distance. I walk straight in.

A motion sensor clicks on the main light, and I take a seat at the newest computer. His tracking program can find Solana. As long as she's wearing her heart necklace, the map should show us right where she is. Was she wearing the necklace this afternoon? I think so. I hope so. And I hope she didn't throw hers in a pond.

The chair is too high and wide, so I sit up on my knees and jiggle the mouse, lighting up the screen. The username is already entered: TXInstrumentsMacLellan. Below that is a blank box. Password.

Oh, no. What is his password?

I've actually learned some tricks around the security of his old computers, but this computer is new. It has updates and patches, and no way to bypass this screen. Would it be something with his wife's name? His daughter's? I don't even know her name. I don't know his birthday either, though his Nahual, the Earth, pops into my head.

Maybe it's a phrase he uses a lot, a slogan, or one of his science quotes. I look at the posters lining the wall. The faces look back as if they wish they could help. Albert Einstein, Rosalind Franklin, Stephen Hawking, Marie Curie, Carl Sagan, Katherine Johnson. A word floats through my head. "Curiosity." Then half a sentence. "To make an apple pie . . ." How did the rest of it go? "You must first invent the universe."

I lower my head, propping it up with my hand. This is never going to work. It could be anything.

But no, Luz, it's not just anything. It's something significant, or something easy to remember.

I look around the room, hoping to see a slip of paper with the password on it or some writing that stands out.

All I see are computers, motherboards, tools on a pegboard, cables hanging in coils. Boxes of screws, boxes of nails. Stacks of sandpaper and the workbench. A room full of everything Mr. Mac.

That's it! You build a self. He's done it, right here. "The self is not discovered, but created." It does seem a little long, but it's perfect for Mr. Mac.

I type it in with no spaces. Incorrect.

I type it all lowercase, then all uppercase. Incorrect. Incorrect.

This has to be it, I know it. I type the phrase again, this time with underscores between each word. I click ENTER, and the screen takes longer to change this time. It goes black for a split second, and then I'm in.

46

"**Come on, come on, come** *on*," I say to the computer screen as it loads. Solana could be lost by now or sitting on the cold concrete in the dark. She could be hurt or someone could—no. Just get to the tracker and find her.

I click open the Files folder and scan the list. There are about ten versions of ConnorTracker. I look at the dates. Some are a month old or more, and they say "draft." I click the most recent one. That has to be it.

The program opens like a web page—yes! The screen asks me which tracker I want to find—1, 2, 3, 4 or 5. Uh . . . which one is Solana's? I'm guessing Connor's is number one. A couple of unused trackers lie in a ziplock bag on the desk. I check each one. Yes, they're four and five. And then there's mine. I touch my palm to my chest. Where's mine?

My pocket! Thank goodness I didn't throw it into the pond. I pull it out and turn it over. Number two. That means Solana's is three.

I select 3, then hold my breath as I click ENTER.

Immediately, the computer beeps, and the screen flashes. The screen I was on disappears, and the program's code cascades down the screen. `ERROR: MISSING RETURN STATEMENT`.

No, no, no! Tears spring to my eyes. How can there be an error? It worked just a couple of days ago. We tested it on the egg carton. It was done. How can it be broken now?

I try to breathe. I try to set aside my panic and remember that day. We stuck the tracker to the egg carton. We came back and saw it on-screen. Mr. Mac was happy that it worked. What else did he say? *Think, Luz, think!*

He was going to add one thing, that's right. Connor's face! The code about Connor's face has to be the part that's not working.

I look at the cascade of code. I've seen it before. Mr. Mac showed me his indents. He said all the lines indented the same amount are on a team. So there must be a team of lines that refer to Connor's image. If I could find them, I could strip them out, and the code would run like before. Right?

I think it through again. There's probably a fancier way to do it, like a command to detour around that code, but I don't know it.

And there could be another problem. The old part and the new part might be tangled together. Some part of the good code could depend on the broken part.

Still, it's the best chance we have of finding Solana quickly. Mr. Mac, please forgive me for messing with your program. I hope you can code it again.

I scroll quickly, trying to see where the Connor part might be. Mr. Mac has titled his sections—*Thank you!* Signal, Maps, Triangulation, Display. Even with titles, my confidence is waning. The screens go on and on. My Showcase program is an anthill compared to this Mount Everest.

Finally I come to a piece of code that's indented deeply. Its lines start halfway across the screen. I study the commands and variables Mr. Mac is using. Set off in a different color, I see JPG, the file type for an image. This could be it. I don't recognize the commands around it, but this whole team of lines is in a section called Location.

My hand hesitates to highlight and delete. *It's already broken,* I tell myself. *I'm not killing it.* Wait—isn't there a way to comment it out? Was it slashes? Never mind. I highlight the JPG section and cut the code instead of deleting. I paste it into a notepad program, so Mr. Mac doesn't have to retype it later.

I may have fixed it, or I may have broken it more. By now the sky is truly dark, black as the ICE vehicle's tinted windows.

I run the program, and again it shows me the tracker numbers. Again, I type in "3." Again, the screen flashes. But this time, a map unfurls across the screen. And, blinking toward the right side, a red dot.

Relief and gratitude flood my body, and my cheeks moisten with slow tears.

Shouting reaches my ears. "Luz! Luz!"

Mom and Dad slam out the door across the street. I hear their pounding footsteps in the dark. Then they are towering above me in the garage's light, breathing hard, faces flushed. Dad scoops me up like when I was little and hugs me hard, pressing the breath out of me and kissing the top of my head.

"Oh, Luz, Luz," Mom says. "We thought we'd lost you again!" Her voice cracks, and over Dad's shoulder, I can see her body trembling.

"I'm here, I'm here," I say, wanting to erase their worry. "I'm sorry I left without telling you."

Dad sets me down, but holds my shoulders like he's afraid I'll disappear.

"Why in the world did you come here?" Mom asks. "You said Solana left."

"I found her," I say.

"You what?" Dad asks.

"She's wearing a tracker. The heart necklace—it has a tracker on it. Number three. I fixed the tracking program, and that's her!" I say, pointing to the screen.

Dad blinks in confusion. "Are you telling us that this screen shows where Solana is?"

"Yes! I have a tracker too, because . . ." Mom and Dad rush to the screen and study it. "The red dot. That's where she is."

"How do we zoom in on this thing?" Dad says, search-
ing the computer screen. His eyes keep going back to the
blinking red dot. The dot we hope is Solana.

"Emilio, the police." Mom points across the street. A
police car is pulling up in front of our house, and she heads
over.

"Stay right here, Luz," Dad says.

"I'm not going anywhere, Dad." He lingers even as Mom
starts waving down the officers.

Soon I hear the officers' voices, clipped and clear. I can't
make out the conversations, but they take Mom and Dad's
flurry of words and make it into short sentences.

In a minute, they are standing over me, their badges
shining under the garage light. They look like twins in their
matching uniforms, but one is taller.

"Hi, Luz," says the taller officer. "Your parents tell us
that you may know where your sister went?"

"Yes, officer. She's wearing a tracker—at least she *was*." With a little gut-punch, I realize it's probably been hours since she saw the ICE truck and bolted. "As long as she didn't take her necklace off," I say, alarmed that I didn't think of this before. I almost threw my necklace into the pond. What if she did something like that? Or gave it to someone? I think of the dog running around with the egg carton when we tested the tracking program. I hope that dot really is her.

"Is this the tracking system?" the other officer says, stepping forward.

"Yes, Mr. Mac's program," I say.

"Who is Mr. Mac?" the taller officer says to my parents. They explain that we're in his garage. "Is he inside? Do you have permission to be on the premises?"

"Yes, he gave me this note and his garage door opener," I say, handing them the envelope.

"Officers, please." Dad grips his hair with both hands. "I'd like to find my daughter as soon as possible."

"Of course, Mr. Véliz, but we have to make sure of these things."

"Yes, I understand," Dad says.

The officer at the computer taps the screen. "It looks like this dot is at the ball field, at the other end of this jogging trail here." We all gather around the screen. "Doesn't this look like the trail?" he says.

"And where are we?" Mom asks.

We have to scroll up to find a rooftop that must be our house.

"That must be nearly ten miles from here," Dad breathes. "Could she really be that far away?"

The shorter officer says, "The average pedestrian walks three or four miles per hour. And she's been missing how long?"

Mom and Dad look at each other. "About three hours?" Mom guesses.

"What are we waiting for?" I ask. "Let's go!"

The officers stand side by side, and I read their name tags: LOPEZ and LEWIS. "We'll go check out the signal. You folks should stay here," they say. "In case she shows up."

"No!" I shout, and immediately regret yelling at police officers. "I'm very sorry. I mean, Solana is scared. If she sees your uniforms, she might hide or run off again."

Officer Lopez talks to Officer Lewis. "You take Mom or Dad with you. I'll stay here and watch the computer screen."

Everyone moves, like a spell has broken. Dad and Officer Lewis go one direction, and Mom comes to stand beside me. Officer Lopez leans over the computer screen.

"Can't I go?" I ask Mom.

"Sweetheart, it's probably better if—"

"Luz!" Dad calls. "Come with us! She'll want to see you."

Mom squeezes my hand and nods, showing she agrees. I silently thank Dad. I'm sure he's the one who asked Officer Lewis to let me come.

Soon we're in Dad's loud pickup, since it's parked on the street and unhitched from the mowing trailer. The police car takes the lead, and we follow to the ball field. *Don't move, Solana. We're coming!*

Dad's truck *clunkety-clunks* into the ball field's parking lot, and I scan the dark field for any sign of Solana. A full moon would help, but we'll have to see by the light of the grocery store parking lot across the street.

"I bet she's in one of the dugouts," Dad says, pointing to two covered awnings.

We jump out of the truck and call, "Solana!"

I walk as fast as I can toward the first-base dugout.

"Be careful in this dark, Luz," Dad calls. The dugouts are not actually dug out of the ground, but just benches set up under the awnings. "She's not here," I yell to Dad, who's run to the other dugout.

"Not here either," Dad says.

Officer Lewis talks into his radio, then walks onto the field.

"They're not going to deport you," I shout. The darkness seems to swallow my voice. "We want you to come home!"

A motorcycle whizzes by on the street, and Officer Lewis's radio crackles.

"I miss you," I say, softer this time.

"She could have left this spot by now," Officer Lewis says.

Unhelpful, if you ask me, but I have to admit it's true.

Dad takes a few steps toward the Bark Park, a yard for dogs, when a rustling noise comes from a wooded area beyond third base. I can barely make out a metal picnic table under the trees. Below the table, a shadow moves, and I think it must be a dog, escaped from one of the yards nearby. But when the shadow stands up, I know it's her.

"Solana!" I take off at an almost-run.

We meet in a hug, and I hold her hard, squeezing with all my might.

In a second, Dad's arms wrap around us both, and for that moment and the next and the next, nothing exists but the love between us. The force of it fills my ears with a roar, like the ocean. It feels like we're glowing with an energy that could power all the lights of the world.

Finally, Dad lets us go and calls Mom on his cell phone. "She's here!" he tells her. "They're both here."

I look into Solana's eyes. "I was so scared for you."

"The black truck, Luz. I think of Rodrigo and I run and run."

"The truck frightened me, too," I say.

"Why they come?" She still looks worried, like they might come back. "And him?"

I follow her gaze to Officer Lewis, standing by the squad car.

"He's helping us find you. And the black-truck guys—they took a survey, is all. Just easy questions. No arresting."

Solana's shoulders relax. "I am being so sorry about the computer program of yours."

"*I'm* sorry." It occurs to me how happy I am that I can stand here in front of her and apologize. "I yelled at you in front of your friends. And I said some terrible things. Solana, I didn't mean them. I promise I didn't. I'm so glad you came here. I'm so glad we are sisters."

She takes my face in both her hands, squeezing my cheeks in a face hug.

"And something else." I take a deep breath because I want to get this right. "I've learned from you. You value everyone, no matter what. I didn't think that way before. Now I get it."

Solana smiles, looking like she's known I would learn this. "But your Scratch, Luz. I wish everything be okay," she says.

"It wasn't your fault. Look." I hold up the note from Mr. Mac. I guess I've been clutching it ever since the police officer gave it back to me. "Mr. Mac even says it wasn't. Anyway, all that matters is that *you're* okay."

As we bump home in the truck, Solana and I hold hands. I show her Mr. Mac's letter, and she reads about the Parkinson's. "Medicine helps!" she shouts over the truck noise. I nod and give a thumbs-up.

When Mom sees us, she bursts into tears and lifts Solana off the ground in a tight hug.

"I am happissima," Solana says.

I know exactly what she means. I'm extra happy, too.

We thank the police officers, turn off the computer, and close up Mr. Mac's garage.

At home, we all collapse on comfy chairs and couches in the living room. "This calls for something special," Dad says.

"But it's almost midnight," Mom yawns.

"How about hot *chocolate*?" Dad hasn't stopped smiling, and now his eyes shine extra bright.

"You mean hot chocolate?" I ask.

"No, *chocolate*," he repeats, saying it the Spanish way.

Solana clarifies. "Not white paper bag."

"Not the powder kind? In the packets?"

She shakes her head. "Brown circles from el mercado. In the . . . cómo se dice . . ."

"Pantry! Yes!" I say. I've seen them. The round, hard, pancake-looking things. I've been wondering about those. "How do we make it?"

"Just break off a piece and melt it in milk," Mom says. "And add cinnamon!" She doesn't look a bit tired now.

Over frothy mugs and cinnamon sticks, we talk quietly, reliving the whole evening. I tell everyone about my trip to the pond, and Solana tells us how the ICE seal made her freeze in the middle of the street before running to the trail.

"I am again sorry about your computer program, Luz."

I shake my head. "I don't even care about that anymore, hermana," I say. "You're more important than any program."

"And so are you," Dad says to me.

I take in his open face, his calm smile. He means it. I'm important. Just sitting here.

"You girls mean the world to me," he says.

"To both of us," says Mom, taking Dad's hand.

I don't need cheers to know it's true.

Wednesday morning's sunlight shines through our curtains. With a start, I realize that I must be late for school.

I scurry down the bunk-bed ladder and stumble into the kitchen.

Dad's sipping coffee and reading the newspaper on his tablet. "I thought I'd let you sleep in, get you over to school at ten or so. You still have about an hour."

Whew. "Thanks, Dad!" And what a surprise! This is the great thing about Dad being his own boss of Véliz Verde. He can start work when he wants and also take Solana and me to school. Mom's already in her band hall, I'm sure. "I've never been late to school on purpose before."

"Well, it was a late night, wasn't it?" He puts his tablet facedown on the table. "And a special one."

We share a hug.

"Luz, I need to tell you something." He keeps hold of my hand. "Last night, I was worried out of my mind. The last time I was worried like that—well, you probably know."

"When I got hurt?"

"Yes. You said I stopped doing things with you. That we stopped spending time together even before Solana came. I thought about it, and you're right. After the accident, I left you alone."

Is he saying what I think he's saying? I step closer.

"I've been thinking about why, and I want to tell you. The thing is, I felt like it was my fault."

"The accident? How?"

He sighs. "Well, I pushed you so hard. I made you practice and go out for the League team."

"But I liked it," I say. "And I was good."

"I know. You were. But I took it so seriously. I wanted it too much. And that day, that run? I told you to run faster, remember? I yelled out, and you sped up, and that's right when it happened. If I hadn't . . ." He presses his forehead with his fingers and closes his eyes.

"Dad, it's okay."

He takes a deep breath, and then looks me in the eye. "I never want you to think that your talent is more important than *you*. Whether it's for fútbol or computers or anything else."

Adults don't apologize much, I've noticed. They never want to be wrong. But sometimes they surprise you.

"Thanks, Dad."

"I love you, kiddo." He reaches out and messes up my hair.

"I love you, too." We bump fists. Bright sun shines around the room.

"Do I smell waffles?" I say.

"You do, Lucita. *Waff-less*, I used to call them in Spanglish." His eyes twinkle.

"I'll get dressed and be right back!" In the bedroom, I use a singsong voice to gently wake Solana. "Solana . . . Waffles . . ."

"Waffles?" she says right away.

"You were already awake!" I give her a gentle arm punch. We both laugh.

> > >

The whole day, I walk around in a good mood. Which is a little odd, considering that I have to give up some lunch time to tell Ms. Freeman about my Scratch code being wiped out by a computer virus. As I give back the robot she let me practice with, I tell her I'll be seeing her in Robotics 1 next year, not 2. Somehow it doesn't even matter that much.

"I'd love to have you attend the Showcase and see the other projects," Ms. Freeman says.

"Of course. You know that Trevor *still* won't reveal what his will be?"

She laughs.

"So I *have* to come, to see for myself and cheer him on."

"I'm so glad you found us this year, Luz," Ms. Freeman says.

"I am, too. I've learned a bucketful of Scratch commands and how they work. And hanging out at the club has been awesome."

"I think you've grown some, too, Luz."

I stand up straight, thinking she means that I'm taller.

"No, I mean you've matured. You'll be a valuable part of the club next year."

I feel my ears turning warm. "Thanks, Ms. Freeman."

I pat R2-D2 as I leave, and head to lunch. But I see that the hall is not empty. Alicia's drinking at the water fountain. Alicia, who wouldn't be my partner a long time ago. Alicia, who is now Solana's friend and saw my meltdown at Mr. Mac's.

"Hey," I say, with a chin lift and a smile.

A slight frown passes across her face, and she gives me a tiny wave.

I don't blame her. The last time she saw me, I was chewing out her friend and generally being the Worst Sister Ever.

I close the gap between us before she scurries away. "Um, Alicia?"

She looks at me warily.

"How are you?"

"Okay," she says evenly, moving a book and a folder from one arm to the other.

Do better, Luz! "Here's the thing. I want to apologize. I lost my temper the other day."

She nods.

"And I haven't been kind to you. Or Mariana or Lorena either. I'm really sorry."

Now her face softens. "This is the first time you talk to me, Luz."

My neck goes hot. She's right. "I guess I didn't know if you'd understand."

"I understand you very well," she says, raising one eyebrow.

Oh, boy. All that annoyance I thought I was hiding wasn't hidden after all. Every time I thought they were rude, I'm guessing *I* was. I pull on my ear, not sure what to do with my embarrassment.

She leans toward me. "Luz, maybe we are friends now?"

I'm not sure why she would want to be friends with me, but I tell her the truth. "I'd like that."

"Solana say you have a good heart. Now I start to believe her."

My feelings are a spaghetti bowl. I can't believe I treated her so badly and almost missed out on being her friend. Regret and relief mix with gratitude. Somehow, Solana had faith in me all along.

I meant it when I said I'm learning from my sister. I'm learning a lot.

"Mom, can I use one of your hair thingies?" My hair is getting long enough that it's hot on my neck. The morning is already warm and what Mom calls muggy. She means the air is heavy and wet feeling.

"Sure, there's one on my dresser," she calls.

I find the elastic band and pull my hair into a stubby ponytail. Solana approves and adds some clips on the sides to catch the shorter hairs that want to escape. I think it makes me look older.

As we leave the house to catch the bus to school, I hear a familiar metallic noise. I'd know that sound anywhere. It's Mr. Mac's garage door!

"Hey, Mr. Mac!"

"My lights across the street!"

"That's us!" I say. The bus won't come for fifteen minutes or more. I look at Solana to confirm, and we trot over together.

"Mr. Mac, we miss to see you!" Solana says.

"I missed you too, girls."

"How was the doctor, Mr. Mac?" I ask. "I didn't know you'd be back today."

"You're kind to ask, Luz. I'm getting some medication to help with those tremors. And I should sleep better, too."

"It sounds like Stephen Hawking would be proud."

"Eh?"

"'Intelligence is the ability to adapt to change'?"

He chuckles. "Quite right, Luz. Quite right. May I say, it's good to see you smiling!"

"Well, I guess you could say . . ." I'm not sure how to put this. "I got over all my mad. I'm just glad that Solana's here, and that I'm here. And that *you're* here." It sounds a little mushy, but Mr. Mac smiles, his cheeks almost boosting up his round glasses.

"You girls are on your way to school, I see, so I'll be quick. But I have something to show you."

He ducks into the garage, and we follow.

When he takes a seat in front of the virus-infected computer, I wonder if he's confused.

"Isn't this the dead computer?" I ask.

"It's not completely dead. It's sick, all right, but I was able to use the command prompts to retrieve some files from the hard drive."

"Retrieve? Mr. Mac, are you saying . . ."

"I'm saying that I found your code, Luz."

I'm frozen to the spot where I'm standing.

Solana understands because she claps and makes a little jump. "Good news, good news!" she says.

"It *is* good news," I say. "Are you sure, Mr. Mac?" It's almost too great to be real.

"It's right here," he says.

And so it is. The colored command blocks stack on top of each other just as I had them. The commands for the graphics cluster in their spot. The word lists are intact. I even see the Wait Block in its new position, right where I moved it for the final version.

"I don't even know what to say," I breathe.

"How about 'Here's my flash drive.'" Mr. Mac winks. "Or actually, I'll transfer this to a safe computer first." He sends the file through email to his laptop.

I dig out my flash drive, and in about one minute, Solana and I are walking to the bus with the entire program in my pocket. Maybe her feet are touching the pavement, but I'm walking on air.

We take the hump seat on the bus, and as the engine lurches into gear, I put together what this means. I have something for the Showcase. Ms. Freeman and Trevor can see the CheerBot and try out my GrowBot game. I can show people Solana's graphics.

And it's all happening *tonight.*

51

Solana holds my hand as we enter the school library at 7:00 p.m. sharp, followed by Mom and Dad, who are holding hands, too. We pass through a curtain of blue and white streamers into a room that buzzes with activity. The tables stand in clusters, and each one holds a computer or a robot or both. Kids set up their projects, and grown-ups wander from table to table greeting other parents, grandparents, and friends.

Ms. Freeman waves, her bright sleeves billowing around her. She weaves her way toward us between tables. This morning, I gave her the news that Mr. Mac resurrected my program.

"You'll be at Table Four, Luz. I'm so glad you're here! And Solana, our animator and graphics designer! Good to have you. And this must be your family."

Ms. Freeman talks with our parents while Solana and I slip over to Table 4. A card on the table says LUZ VÉLIZ-GROWBOT AND CHEERBOT in a blocky font.

This is it. The chance I prepped for all spring. I thought I'd be nervous, like before a soccer game, but I'm not at all. Maybe because whichever way this goes, I'm happy. The worst thing that could happen already did. It's great just to be here.

I load up my code from my flash drive while Solana turns on the robot. "Let's make sure he's receiving commands through Bluetooth," I say.

"Luz! Solana!" Trevor shouts. "Come see my bot!"

"Trevor!" Solana waves.

"Be right there!" I say, pressing the power button on the brick and doing a quick test. "Everything's a go here," I tell Solana. "Come on."

We thread through the tables and groups of people to get to Trevor. He wears a shirt that shows a hand drawing a hand, which is drawing the original hand. It reminds me of Mr. Mac's fractals. "Cool shirt," I say. I'm glad he'll be here next year, a familiar face in the club, especially since Solana will go on to high school. It's dawning on me now how much I'll miss her being here.

"The secret is revealed!" Trevor says. "Here's my robot. A Segway Rider!"

He balances it carefully, then lets it go. As we watch the bot roll down the table on two wheels, Solana whispers something to herself in Spanish. I hear the awe in her voice. It really does look like those Segways that tourists and sometimes police officers ride around town.

"But why doesn't it fall over?" I ask. "It's balancing perfectly. Does it use a gyroscope like the real ones?"

"Nope," Trevor says, smiling.

I take a closer look. The brick forms a base, with two motors and wheels, like a two-wheeled car. Above that, a vertical motor creates a body with some beams for arms, and a little head decorates the top. Then I see it! The ingenious part is a color sensor plugged into the brick near the bottom. Its light points straight down at the table.

"Does it measure how much light is reflected off the table?" I ask.

"You guessed it," Trevor says. "That's why I covered the table in white paper. So it can get a good reading."

What a great idea. The whole bot balances by adjusting to keep the amount of light the same. Leaning forward or back changes the light, and the wheels move to correct it.

"This is truly cool, Trevor."

Solana gives the bot a gentle push backward. It leans a bit, then corrects itself. "Impressive!" she says.

"Her English is better than mine sometimes," Trevor says, shaking his head.

"I know, right?" I say. "A lot of hard words sound almost the same in Spanish. So she knows more hard words than I do."

"That's crazy! Hey, Luz, where's your bot?" Trevor looks out across the room.

"Table Four," I say. "Come and see."

Solana catches my eye and motions that she's going to check out the rest of the room. "Have fun," I say.

As Trevor and I get closer to Table 4, I notice a familiar figure standing there. "Skyler?"

"Hi, Luz. Who's this?"

I wonder why she's here, but I don't have a chance to ask. "This is Trevor," I say. "He's in Robotics Club."

"Hey," she says, and Trevor nods.

"You should see his Segway Rider robot!" I say.

"Wow, I will. What does your robot do?" she asks me.

"I'll show you." I wiggle the mouse, and the screen lights up. "Honored guests," I say in a bad British accent. "May I present Cheerleader Robot, or CheerBot, who reacts to your progress in my Build-a-Robot game, which I call GrowBot."

"Let's see," Skyler says, reading the screen. "Guess a letter to the mystery word." She studies the bare robot torso on the screen and the conveyor belt. "So what happens if I guess right?"

"A new part gets added to the robot," I say.

Trevor leans over her shoulder. "Try *E*. It's the most common letter."

"Mm-kay." Skyler types *E*, and CheerBot says, "Uh-oh!" The conveyor belt lurches forward. "Oh, man! Now it's closer to this—what is it? A flaming recycle bin?"

"I like it, Luz," Trevor says.

"I'm going to try *A*," Skyler says.

This time, a robot part is added, and CheerBot raises both arms, saying, "Good job!"

Skyler looks at it. "It's talking!"

"And moving," Trevor adds. "So you programmed it to respond to the game outcomes."

"Exactly."

"Let's get them all wrong and see what happens," Trevor says.

"No way! I'm winning this thing," Skyler says.

Part by part, the robot gets built. Soon she's guessing the final letter.

"Way to go!" says CheerBot as its legs move in a marching motion, and its arms lift and lower. The dance ends with a trumpet fanfare.

"My turn!" Trevor says.

It's fun to watch them enjoy something I made. Even if Ms. Freeman doesn't let me join the advanced class, this is a great night.

As they finish up game number seven or eight, I say to Skyler, "I'm surprised to see you here, Sky."

"Oh, my mom volunteers for this event. She works at Bell Helicopter. So Ms. Freeman asked me to help move chairs and tables and stuff. Set up, you know."

"I had no idea your mom was into helicopters," I say. "I bet that's an awesome job."

"She's into it, all right," Skyler says. "An engineer. See-ing all this kinda makes me understand why."

"It is cool to see all the projects," I agree. "Thanks for playing my game."

"CheerBot! He's the best part." She smiles and says, "See you around?"

"Sure." I say. "I'll come to a game one of these days."

She gives me a thumbs-up and heads off to see the other projects.

I turn back to my Table 4. "Trevor, you're still here!"

"I'm trying to see how many words you put in here. Is it like, twenty?"

"You'll have to play all night to find out," I tease.

"Ahhh!" He makes a big show of clutching his chest in agony. "Where's Solana, by the way?" he asks.

"Around here somewhere." I'm not surprised that he's asking about her. I think it's time to say the obvious. "I, uh, know you like her."

"What?" He looks up from the keyboard.

"It's too bad she'll be at the high school next year."

"No, Luz."

"It won't be too bad?"

He shakes his head. "No, I mean, I like *you.*" He makes a small choking sound. "I didn't mean for it to come out that way."

"Wait, what?"

"Well, of course she's great and all, but I just talked to her to find out more about you."

My head goes dizzy as I try to put this together. "You mean you hung around Solana to . . ."

"Yeah." He looks at the floor.

"Oh." I think back to his ease with Solana and his nervousness with me. I guess it makes more sense.

"But if you . . ." He looks worried.

"No, I . . . I like you, too." I smile a new kind of smile.

Trevor's face relaxes, and his dark eyes shine. "So do we, like, uh . . . ?"

"I don't know," I say. "I guess we'll just, you know, see each other at club and stuff."

"Yeah. And lunch. And I bet you'll be in my Robotics class."

"Ms. Freeman will decide tonight," I say.

"She's gonna love this, Luz."

"I hope so."

For a moment we just stand in the quiet, a comfy quiet.

"I better get back to my Segway."

"Later?" I say, holding up my fist for a bump.

He meets it in the air. "Later."

The evening is almost over, and Mom, Dad, and Solana have circled back to me. They've enjoyed all the projects.

At last Ms. Freeman comes to Table 4 for the judging. This is it. I wasn't nervous before, but now I feel my hands go a little sweaty. I start to explain CheerBot and the game, but Ms. Freeman stops me. "Let me figure it out, like a real user would. You can't always be around to explain your programs, right?"

I see her point.

I watch as she types in guesses and CheerBot reacts. I've programmed enough sad sounds that they don't repeat. Same with the happy ones. She deliberately misses a word to watch the on-screen robot fall into the flaming recycle bin. Then she gets the next word right and sees the finished robot jump off the assembly line. CheerBot dances and belts out its fanfare.

Finally she turns to me. "Luz, your skills have come a long way. You should be very proud of that. You're using custom sound files, graphic changes that update with user results, and iterative code. And you know your way around a brick." She pauses to make eye contact and hitch an eyebrow. "While you could learn a few things in Robotics One, I think you're ready for the advanced class."

I let her words sink in. *Ready for the advanced class.* I hear her voice over and over until I believe it. I have an urge to call and tell Mr. Mac. It was his teaching that gave me the biggest push. And then there was Solana, who helped me with Scratch when I first started. Trevor gave me pointers on the robot. Mr. Sung helped me learn basic bot commands, and Ms. Freeman provided the club. This took a whole team. "Thanks, Ms. Freeman. I couldn't have done it without the club and that intro class, and so many of you." Solana may be right; there are upsides to being around people.

"And you, the new high school freshman," Ms. Freeman says to Solana. "I'm giving your name to the computer graphics teacher up there. He'll be on the lookout for you. Luz told me this morning that you made these images for her game, and I saw your quetzal animation during club time. You have a knack for graphic design. Think about developing that."

Dad steps in to translate, but I think Solana understood most of it. She's standing tall, and shining like the sunny person she is.

"What a fine pair of girls you have, Mr. and Mrs. Véliz," Ms. Freeman says.

"We couldn't agree more," Mom says.

"Exactly right," Dad agrees.

"See you next year, Luz." Ms. Freeman meets my eyes again and suddenly, I feel raised, lifted, hoisted, off the floor.

"Let's get a picture!" Dad says. "Luz, stand between the computer screen and CheerBot." He clicks a few times.

"Now one with Solana!" I say. I pull Solana next to me, and Dad takes a few more.

"I know!" Solana says. "One with the hearts."

Sure enough, we're both wearing our heart necklaces. We hold them up and put our heads together, and Dad steps in to take a close-up.

"That's a beautiful one," Mom says.

"Let's send it to Mr. Mac," I say, and Solana hops, gripping my arm.

"Yes, yes!" she says.

"What should I caption it?" Dad says.

Solana's eyes meet mine, and we say it together: "Your lights across the street."

Luz + Solana's Inspiration Board

Stephen Hawking (1942-2018) English theoretical physicist, cosmologist, and author. "Intelligence is the ability to adapt to change."

Carl Sagan (1934-1996) American astronomer, astrophysicist, astrobiologist, author, and popular science personality. "To make an apple pie, you must first invent the universe."

Marie Curie (1867-1934) Polish-French physicist and chemist. "Nothing is to be feared, it is only to be understood. Now is the time to understand more, so that we may fear less."

Albert Einstein (1879-1955) German-American theoretical physicist. "I have no special talents. I am only passionately curious."

Paula Nicho Cúmez (1955-) Mayan-Guatemalan artist, painter of *Crossing Borders*.

Solana's Chilaquilas

- 3 güisquiles (also called chayotes or pear squash), cut into slices ½ inch (12 millimetres) thick
- 4 eggs
- 8 ounces queso fresco (also called queso blanco), cut into slices ¼ inch (6 millimetres) thick
- 4 tablespoons cooking oil
- Tomato salsa, for garnish
- Cilantro, for garnish
- Cheese, for garnish
- Rice, for serving (optional)

1. Boil the güisquil slices in salted water to soften, but do not over-soften; make sure they stay stiff enough to pick up.

2. Beat the eggs in a medium bowl until thickened, even frothy, about 5 minutes (an electric mixer helps!).

3. Put a slice of queso fresco between two slices of güisquil. Use all slices to make "squash-cheese sandwiches."

4. One at a time, dip the chilaquilas deep into the eggs to fully coat.

5. Heat the cooking oil in a large frying pan over medium-high heat.

6. Fry each chilaquila until golden brown, about 5 minutes each side. Set on a paper towel–lined plate.

7. When serving, top with warm tomato salsa and cilantro or cheese. Good with rice!

Guatemalan Hot Chocolate

- 1-2 ounces of Guatemalan or Mexican chocolate (tablets of sweetened, pressed cocoa, which are dry and crumbly)
- 1 cup of milk
- a cinnamon stick (or a few dashes of powdered cinnamon)

1. In a saucepan, simmer these ingredients until the sugar from the chocolate dissolves. (A microwave works, but watch that the milk doesn't overflow.)

2. Pour into a wide mug.

3. Whisk until frothy. It is traditional to say "Ba-te, ba-te, cho-co-la-te" as you roll the whisk back and forth between your hands.

Author's Note

My stories are houses of fiction built on a foundation of fact. That is, I often build the imaginary on something real.

I met my real Guatemalan half sister for the first time when we were both adults. Our father had learned of her existence only the year before. Though we speak different languages and live in different countries, we've laughed over many stories and shared unforgettable adventures. I'm sure she won't forget the time I took her line dancing at a Texas honky-tonk! Sadly, stricter rules about immigration have made it harder for her to visit in person, but we hope that can change.

Unfortunately, the violence in Guatemala is also all too real. In one of our visits, I got to know my aunt's brother, who we called Meño. He was a knowledgeable guide, driving us to see a sacred lake and hike a volcano. Only a month after that trip, we received shocking news: Meño had been shot. At some point, he had crossed paths with a gang, and they had been waiting to take revenge. I can still see his broad smile. May he rest in peace.

Some Guatemalans flee to other countries. My uncle was one of these, escaping death threats from the political party he spoke out against by immigrating to Canada, which offered him and his family safety. Others aren't so fortunate. Hundreds of thousands of Central Americans have fled their homes. Some wait in long lines or on months-long waiting lists to apply for asylum at the US border. Then they wait more months or even years, sometimes in unsafe conditions, to have their cases decided by a judge. Families who cross the border without going through this process present themselves to border patrol agents who place them in detention centers. These centers can be heartbreakingly inhumane places.

In my story, Solana is able to avoid all of this because of a rare, lucky situation—her father is a United States citizen. She is able to find safety in her father's home.

I'm happy to say that my real-life sister is safe, and that she lives a satisfying life in Guatemala. One of her daughters is a teacher and the other one is a lawyer. My wish is for violence to end and for all Guatemalans to thrive in safety. Que Dios los bendiga.

Acknowledgments

A full spectrum of people contributed their attention, expertise, and love to make this book glow.

Meteor showers of thanks to my radiant agent, Katie Grimm; my incandescent editor, Taylor Norman; cover artist star, Caribay Marquina; and the brilliant Chronicle constellation of Jay Marvel, Kevin Armstrong, Claire Fletcher, Lucy Medrich, Andie Krawczyk, Eva Zimmerman, Mary Duke, Anna-Lisa Sandstrum, and Carrie Gao.

Sparkles of appreciation to my many feedback partners, and especially beta reader Trich, who illumines dim corners of my drafts and my days.

Special thanks to immigration attorney Lauren Glass-Hess for enlightening me on how visas and citizenship work, and Marie Marqardt, who put me in touch with her.

A spotlight for my son Matthew, who gave feedback, talked through game possibilities, and then coded Luz's game in Scratch. You are my constant light.

Thank you, Grandpa Cram, Uncle Bruce, and Uncle Chuck, for charging my battery with the wonders of science, workbenches, and tools. I can still smell the sawdust in the shop of Westlawn's basement.

High-watt hugs to Mom and Dad. Always know that your love lights my way.

Thank you, gleaming readers. You make it a privilege to do this work.